For Love of Celia

Also by Elisabeth Kidd

A Hero for Antonia
The LadyShip
My Lord Guardian

For Love of Celia

Elisabeth Kidd

Walker and Company
New York

Copyright © 1988 by Linda Triegel

All rights reserved. No part of this book may be reproduced or transmitted in any form or by any means, electronic or mechanical, including photocopying, recording, or by any information storage and retrieval system, without permission in writing from the Publisher.

All the characters and events portrayed in this story are fictitious.

First published in the United States of America in 1988 by the Walker Publishing Company, Inc.

Published simultaneously in Canada by Thomas Allen & Son Canada, Limited, Markham, Ontario.

Library of Congress Cataloging-in-Publication Data

Kidd, Elisabeth.
    For love of Celia.

    I. Title.
PS3561.I327F67   1988   813'.54
87-37251 ISBN 0-8027-1017-4

Printed in the United States of America.

This one is for Elsa.

1

THERE WERE OCCASIONS when Celia Morland was grateful for the flaw in her character that made her appear to take the most appalling news with almost indecent lack of feeling. True, this made her behaviour open to misinterpretation by more sanguine personalities, but it also served to disguise the consternation she did in fact feel at such news as that which her sister-in-law had just imparted to her. Fortunately, Kitty was so engrossed in what she was saying that she failed to notice Celia's eyes widen in alarm, and by the time she paused for breath her companion's eyes were once again lowered to the fringe she was so industriously knotting.

"I had no notion the Proctors were in England again," Celia remarked in her usual, softly modulated voice, all the while diligently considering the implications of this piece of information.

"Nor had anyone," Kitty answered gaily, patting a fern quite as tall as she was on its topmost fronds.

She had been rereading *The Scottish Chiefs* but had not been able to keep her mind on the page. Instead, she'd asked Celia whether she thought there had been any such castles as described in Mrs. Porter's novel in their part of Britain and what sort of gown she imagined Lady Mar might have worn. Finally, she laid her book down and began to roam around the small room.

She certainly presented a charming picture, Celia thought, as Kitty flitted from one plant in the sun parlour to the next, annointing each with a few drops from a delicately shaped, enamelled watering pot. As there was no one but Celia to admire her, Kitty soon abandoned her pose and her watering pot and deposited herself more comfortably, if less picturesquely, onto a wicker chair.

"I could not have been more astonished," Kitty assured her once again, "to come upon them taking the air on Bridge Street, for all the world as if they had done so every morning of their lives."

Celia looked at Kitty, who was curling the ribbon that hung from the lace trim at the waist of her gown. She dropped the ribbon and began rotating her small shapely foot in its kid slipper first in one direction, then the other. It struck Celia that something more lay behind Kitty's introduction of Sir Phineas and Lady Proctor into the conversation than her usual eagerness to share a choice *on dit* or to embellish anything in the least out-of-the-way to occur in their quiet neighbourhood. It was not at all in Kitty's nature to be devious, and her pretty, candid countenance was normally incapable of concealing even the smallest mystery. Nevertheless, her eyes did not meet Celia's, and her sister-in-law thought she heard an oddly discordant note in Kitty's gay chatter and pressed her gently to see if it might sound again.

"I wonder at their being in Lyme Regis at all," Celia said, continuing as placidly as possible with her fringe. "I should think discretion would have dictated their remaining at a somewhat greater remove from the scene of—well, of their former indiscretion."

"Oh, but that all happened more than thirty years ago!" Kitty exclaimed with youth's blithe unconcern over anything that took place before its time. "Surely one must forgive what is so long past. Besides, I'm sure they could not help themselves. They must have been desperately in love to sacrifice all for it as they did. And what is more, it must have been true love, for has it not stood the test of time?"

Celia smiled at that. She could look back on scarcely four summers more than Kitty's nineteen, but Celia often felt herself more an aunt than a sister-in-law to the younger girl. She had always been the quiet, thoughtful one and perhaps for that very reason had been first drawn to the Morlands' gaity and careless acceptance of whatever life offered them. At seventeen, Celia had even thought this attitude sufficient to ensure her own happiness and had married Kitty's brother Harry on the strength merely—or so it seemed to her now when she paused to wonder over it—of his laughing eyes and unfailingly sunny disposition. Then Harry died, his bright flame extinguished as quickly as it had been kindled; and, had it not been for Kitty, Celia feared she would not now even remember what he looked like.

Still, the Morlands continued to surprise her. Kitty's betrothal to Julian Hardwicke was the last announcement Celia would have expected to hear from her. To be sure, Mr. Hardwicke was one of the most eligible bachelors in the county and could not be faulted for either the size of his fortune or the antiquity of his family line. He was, moreover, a fine-looking man—tall and broad-shouldered and, even in the country, always impeccable in his choice of raiment and never to be seen with either his neckcloth or his curling brown hair in disarray.

Nevertheless, while he was a firm favourite with the local mamas, their daughters found him a little too admirable to be very exciting. Julian was perfectly capable of exercising his authority with confidence and precision, but he profoundly disliked being the centre of anyone's attention himself. This sprang, Celia suspected, from modesty more than misanthropy. However, modesty was not a quality likely to impress young ladies of a hero-worshipping disposition.

Furthermore, although Julian had known Kitty since she was an impish child in pinafore and pantalettes, and they had always been fond of each other, Celia could not help wondering if that would be enough to overcome the fifteen-year gap in their ages and the much greater disparity in their characters—not to mention the dozens of younger beaux whose pursuit of the delectable Miss Morland had abated only slightly since the announcement of her betrothal. Others than Celia had found that announcement difficult to accept.

It was not that Celia was uneager to see Kitty happily settled, but she was still young enough to be impulsive in her choice of a husband. Indeed, Celia was reasonably certain that Kitty had received no other offers. The several aspirants there had been to her hand had come to Celia first for permission to speak to her, but Kitty had not consented to receive any of them.

Poor Mr. Morrison had been reduced to waiting outside church to speak to Kitty, and Mr. Thane had gone so far as to get himself appointed host of the local assembly so that he might dance more than once with her, even though Kitty rarely attended the local assemblies, stigmatising them as infantile. Celia supposed she ought to have been grateful that the task of chaperoning Kitty was made so easy for her, but there was no denying that Kitty had broken hearts before and might yet do so again.

Kitty stretched her slim arms high above her head and lounged inelegantly in her chair. Wisps of her pale golden hair had escaped from her coiffure and blew lazily in the slight breeze that came in from the opened glass doors. The sun parlour was Celia's favourite room at Hardwicke Manor, although it was true that a room could be found there to suit any taste. The manor boasted not only a Norman foundation, confined to the chapel and well concealed by later brickwork, and a Gothic turret added to the west wing by Julian's father, but a sample of every intervening style of architecture. Julian had once remarked that Hardwicke Manor was not merely a landmark, but a spectacle.

The sun parlour—added by a sixteenth-century Hardwicke with an eccentric taste for natural light—featured large, unpaned windows and a sweeping view of Lyme Bay, which on this early May morning shimmered in the sunlight. Little of the town of Lyme Regis, nestled at the foot of the long slope to the sea, could be discerned, and the tip of the famous Cobb was just visible. Manor people could forecast coming storms by the way the waves hit the rocky promontory, but today the sea was calm and sun-dappled. Patches of sunlight played over Kitty's white muslin gown, making her seem more ethereal than ever.

Celia, by contrast, felt all too earthbound. To be sure, her blue silk gown was very becoming to her—one of the privileges of widowhood being release from the need to confine oneself to girlish muslins, which had never flattered her. Her glossy, chestnut hair was bound up neatly in soft waves that emphasised her luminous brown eyes and creamy complexion. Celia loved the sun and the sea as much as Kitty—or Harry, who had been more conscious of it—ever did. Yet, if Kitty was a seabird soaring on the wind above the cliffs, Celia was a lighthouse watching affectionately over such sun-bedazzled creatures while she remained herself firmly anchored to the land.

"But do you think it was quite wise of you to invite them, love?" she admonished Kitty gently, putting her fringe back into her workbasket and taking out of it the most prosaic piece of mending she could find.

Celia felt a need to carry on as if Kitty's announcement that the Proctors would be joining their house party—would, indeed, be arriving the very next morning—had not disconcerted her in the least. Kitty generally greeted any criticism of her behaviour by closing up like the periwinkles on Church Cliffs when the tide was out and Celia wanted very much to hear the entire tale. Then she might consider what had prompted her instinctive apprehension at the introduction of it.

"Well, of course, I had no idea at the time who they were," Kitty said, laying her head back on her arms and closing her eyes. "I fell into conversation with her in the milliner's. When she said that her husband had been a great friend of Julian's father, I invited them on the spot to visit us at the manor. It was only when Sir Phineas came into the shop and introduced himself that I realised what I had done. But—well, they were such sweet old things that I hadn't the heart to make an excuse and retract the invitation. Anyway, Julian's father is dead now, and Julian himself was not even born when Lady Proctor ran off with—I mean, when it all happened. He did not seem at all put out when I told him what I had done. Anyway, Julian would never hold a grudge."

"Nevertheless, it is bound to be a trifle awkward."

"But why? The Danby-Davises are coming as well. You wouldn't know them, but they were bosom-bows of Julian's Aunt Harriet. They are an odd pair of birds, to be sure, but they are of an age with Sir Phineas and Lady Proctor and like them have spent many years in India. So, they must have something in common to talk about."

"Why was Mr. Lambert invited then?" Celia asked. She had been informed in a similar offhand fashion that Julian's friend Nicholas Lambert was in England for the first time in several years and would also be stopping at the manor.

"Nicky?" Kitty said, and Celia was interested to discern a faint blush colour Kitty's cheeks. Celia was not herself acquainted with Mr. Lambert, having been on her honeymoon during his last visit to England. "Oh—well, he evens out the numbers, doesn't he? Anyway, it's always more interesting to have different sorts of people to stay."

Celia said nothing. The house party had been Kitty's idea, agreed to by Julian after she had lamented several times about how dull the country was in the Season, when most of their acquaintance removed to London. For her part, Celia did not find Dorset at all dull. She was aware that her natural resistance to change of any kind might make her seem rather dull herself, so she did her best to hide it, along with her occasional premonitions that too-abrupt change signalled disaster. In any event, she had been installed at the manor at Julian's request, to keep Kitty company, before these ambitious plans were revealed, and Celia could not now contrive an acceptable excuse to take herself back to her own cosy little cottage by the sea.

As the silence lengthened, Kitty opened her eyes to glance

at Celia, then smiled and said slyly, "I invited Nicky for you, of course, goose. He's ever so handsome and charming. Everyone likes him, and even you will succumb. I promise."

"How long will he stay?"

Kitty laughed. "I assure you I will show him the door the instant you tell me you have become bored with him."

Celia resigned herself to yet another of Kitty's matchmaking attempts. Since Kitty's own betrothal, she had become determined that Celia should marry again so that she would not be obliged to live alone when Kitty moved to Hardwicke Manor. Celia had attempted to explain that she would enjoy the solitude and an opportunity to take up her pen again, as she had a modest talent for poetry.

Unfortunately, it was awkward in the extreme to insist upon this without hurting Kitty's feelings by implying that Celia would be happy to see her go. However, since the wedding was yet six months away, Celia hoped that sooner or later she would be accepted as sincere when she said she did not wish to marry again. In the meanwhile, she would simply turn the subject, as she did now by asking Kitty what the Proctors looked like.

"There is a bridal portrait of her in the gallery upstairs," Celia recalled. "It is hidden away in one of the darkest corners, to be sure, but still there. It shows her to have been quite a beauty in her youth. She reminded me rather of you, in the expression of—well, for lack of a better word—joie de vivre. Except of course that Lavinia's hair was red."

Kitty did not answer immediately, and Celia looked to see if she had fallen asleep in the sunshine. Just at that moment a voice coming from across the lawn diverted her attention.

"Oh, here is Nicky now!" Kitty exclaimed—a little too eagerly, Celia thought—as if she were glad of the interruption.

Celia had no time to puzzle over this, for the figure striding towards them soon appeared in the doorway, pausing there for a moment in a graceful attitude as Nicholas Lambert adjusted his eyes to the change of light.

Mr. Lambert, a younger son among several offspring of the gentleman whose property adjoined Hardwicke Manor on the inland side, was indeed a handsome man. He looked younger than his thirty years. His fair hair was becomingly windblown at the moment, but his biscuit-coloured pantaloons and superfine coat, which hinted at a slender yet sturdy figure beneath, showed not a crease. His neckcloth was neatly if not extravagantly tied, and his waistcoat embroidered just enough to lend it interest without appearing gaudy. The sun bronze on his graceful hands and the faint lines at the corners of his hazel eyes and laughing mouth revealed him to be a man at home in the out-of-doors. Nonetheless, his manners were those of one equally comfortable in the highest ton society. Celia was obliged to concede his good looks though, at the moment, his reputed charm was directed solely at Kitty—and unavoidably so since she had jumped up and flung her arms around his neck before he could say a word to either of the ladies.

"Dearest Nicky! I'm so glad you've come."

"Darling Kitten," Mr. Lambert responded, laughing. "I shall go away instantly if you've mussed my cravat!"

He caught Celia's eye for an instant over Kitty's head and raised one delicately arched brow at her as if in mute apology, one adult to another, for the irresistible antics of a favourite child. Celia reluctantly conceded him his charm as well, but apprehension that his presence boded no good would not leave her.

"Oh, pooh!" Kitty said dismissively but pulled away and straightened Mr. Lambert's lapels. Celia noted that he kept his light hold on Kitty's waist. "You know that I particularly wanted you to come."

"I particularly? Why? For my dimpled chin?"

Kitty giggled. "You don't have dimples, silly. Well, just that little sort of dent in your chin," she added, placing her forefinger lightly on the spot in question. "I meant, because you may not be with us very much longer—Julian says you may sail for home any time now the weather's improved—and, well, for your knack at spillikins. I count on you to keep us all amused."

"Do you wonder at my preference for life in the Indies," Mr. Lambert queried rhetorically, "when such is my sadly frivolous reputation in my mother country? But you are forgetting your manners, Kitten, in not having presented me long since to your patient friend who must know you very well, for she does not appear to mind that you have forgotten all about her."

"Oh!" Kitty turned back in sincere consternation to Celia, who had to smile at the obvious truth of Mr. Lambert's accusation. "Oh, dearest, I do beg your pardon. This is Nicky—I mean, Mr. Nicholas Lambert—of Indigo Hill Plantation, Jamaica. Nicky, this is my dearest friend and sister, Celia Morland."

Mr. Lambert let go of Kitty at last, made an elegant bow, and took Celia's hand in a firm but gentle grasp. Observing him thus more closely, Celia thought that he was not so very good-looking after all, at least not in the conventionally accepted way. His nose was a trifle long for his finely boned features and his forehead rather too high. A long scar ran along the back of his right hand, noticeable when he held it out to her. She found herself retaining its grip a little too long before letting go abruptly.

Mr. Lambert, however, revealed no consciousness of her scrutiny. His hazel eyes assessed her as candidly as she did him, but whatever sting there may have been in that acute look was rendered painless by his remarkably sweet smile. Celia was not sure she cared for that smile, which was entirely too disarming.

"I am pleased to make your acquaintance, ma'am," he said simply in a voice unlike that which he used to tease Kitty.

It was as if he adapted his manner to what he conceived most appropriate for the person he was addressing. Not that anyone with the least social address did not do the same, but in Nicky Lambert it seemed to Celia somehow calculating. She made up her mind that she would not like him.

He seemed to sense her wariness, and she was somewhat reassured when he did not immediately attempt to charm her further. Instead, at Kitty's invitation, he took a chair between the two ladies and led the conversation into the conventional impersonal pleasantries, soliciting Celia's opinion on a number of subjects rather than merely offering his own. He had an undeniable ease of address, and she found herself returning answers to his questions quite readily—indeed, even surprising herself by volunteering information he had not solicited.

"My husband was much the same," she said when Mr. Lambert remarked that, although there was nothing he enjoyed more than a day on the water, he had found the long voyage from Jamaica wearisome. "Harry never ventured farther than Exeter, by land or sea, for as long as I knew—"

She stopped suddenly and sent him a mistrustful glance. He smiled and shrugged lightly, as if he regretted having been caught prying into her personal affairs but was unrepentant about what he had learned of them. Celia was unsure whether to resent his skillful manipulation or to be glad that there appeared to be no malice behind it. Kitty interrupted before Celia could quite make up her mind on this point.

"Nicky, guess who is coming here tomorrow."

"I cannot imagine, little one," he assured her, redirecting his attention fully to Kitty. Celia was reluctantly impressed by that ability to shift focus so completely. She herself most often found her attention dissipated several ways at once. "What is more, you will run out of patience before I have made more than two or three wild guesses, so you may as well tell me at once."

"Sir Phineas and Lady Proctor!"

Mr. Lambert looked unexpectedly nonplussed at this intelligence, and it was a moment before he said, "Good God."

"I am so eager to meet them," Kitty went on, as if she had not heard his startled response. "Just think. They are still together after all these years. Is that not an affecting thought?"

"Their being together is not such a wonder when you consider that no one else would associate with them," Mr. Lambert remarked dryly. "Why are they coming here?"

"I invited them," Kitty declared, aware at last that her treat was not universally appreciated.

Celia frowned. Had Kitty's eagerness to *meet* them been only a slip of the tongue? Surely she had said earlier that she had met them in Lyme Regis.

Kitty interpreted her bemused look as further censure and protested, "She is Julian's stepmama, after all—in a manner of speaking—and it seems to me past time to let bygones be bygones."

"We must be grateful, I suppose, that you informed us of their visit at all," Mr. Lambert said. "There would have been a rare bumblebroth had they simply appeared on the doorstep. What precisely do you know of the old scandal, Kitty?"

Kitty's glance drifted off evasively once more, fixing itself on the potted palm in the corner of the room. Mr. Lambert kept his eyes on Kitty, not about to let her evade the question. Celia sat very still, willing herself into near invisibility so that the little drama could play itself to conclusion uninterrupted.

"I know that Lavinia fell hopelessly in love with Phineas and eloped with him to India."

"Despite being married to someone else at the time. Someone who gave her wealth, position, and all the freedom she could possibly wish—and who was her lover's best friend. Did you also know, Kitty, that she tried to obtain a divorce from Julian's father, causing no end of scandal when he would not grant it and dragging all of their names through the mud? It is not surprising that the Proctors had to run as far as India."

"Well, Julian's father should have given her the divorce," Kitty persisted, "instead of making them wait until he was ready to remarry to set them free. I think it is wonderful that she was willing to sacrifice all those sordid, worldly things for a great love."

A tiny muscle twitched beneath Mr. Lambert's ear indicating, Celia feared, fading tolerance rather than amusement at Kitty's impetuous defence of Lady Proctor. Celia judged it time to intervene.

"Perhaps Kitty is right," she said soothingly. "She may be overly romanticising the story, but might it not perhaps be best if we all tried to forgive and forget the past and treated the Proctors as we would any other houseguests? No one of us at the manor now was directly hurt by the scandal, after all."

Mr. Lambert's expression softened as he redirected his engaging smile towards her. "Ah, the voice of moderation is heard. You are quite right, of course, Mrs. Morland."

"Well, isn't that what I have been saying all along?" Kitty objected.

He laughed and pretended to box Kitty's ears, but succeeded only in brushing her cheek lightly with his hand. "It was not what you were *saying*, infant, but what you were *thinking* that had such disturbing potential. Confess now. Were you not hoping that some fresh scandal would result from sowing such a seed in this particular ground, however infertile it must be by now?"

Kitty was indignant. "Nicky, how can you think such a thing?" She glanced sideways at him, as if to soften her words and indicate that she was willing to be cajoled out of her pique.

He coaxed up her chin with his slender fingers and smiled closely into her eyes. "Ah, but I know you, infant. You may not have had any very clear idea of what you intended, but you can never leave well enough alone for very long."

Kitty caught his hand in hers and turned his palm up to trace little patterns on it with her fingertips. "But I never mean anything wicked," she said in a low voice. "You know that, too."

Embarrassed to be a witness to this scene, Celia cast about for a way to make herself visible again. She knew Kitty meant nothing by her flirting, but it had never been one of Celia's pastimes to behave so. She found it difficult to convince herself that Kitty's carrying on was entirely innocent, particularly in view of her assertion that she had invited Nicholas Lambert for Celia's sake. Celia had to be relieved, naturally, that his interest obviously lay elsewhere. Still . . . she ought not to feel so, she knew, but she could not help a little pang that he made his preference for Kitty so apparent.

A movement behind Kitty caught Celia's attention. She looked towards the door leading to the interior of the manor and caught her breath. In the doorway—for how long it was impossible to say, but he had obviously also been a witness to the scene—stood Julian Hardwicke.

2

"Well, hello, Nicky," Julian said, smiling and extending his hand to his friend. "I thought I heard your voice."

Mr. Lambert disregarded the hand, instead throwing his arms around Mr. Hardwicke's shoulders. "Julian, old fellow! How are you? I beg your pardon for descending on you like this, but I rode across country and seem to have beaten my man to your door. He'll be along with my things in time for dinner, I expect."

Julian was conscious of a peevish wish that Nicky would not greet him so heartily, as if he were someone's slightly deaf grandfather. Being aware of the unreasonableness of that thought, Julian did his best to dismiss it by behaving with especial cordiality. "You might have come directly here from London," he admonished Nicky, returning his embrace, "and not had to overnight at Woodbridge."

Nicky grimaced exaggeratedly. "Yes, but you know how it is. Duty calls and so on. I did have to pay my respects to my father, although the poor old soul didn't even recognise me. It's my mother who'd have made me stay if I hadn't had the excuse of your invitation to stop here at the manor.

"Mind you," he added, releasing his hold on Julian in order to move behind Kitty's chair and put his hands on her shoulders while gazing affectionately at her. "If I'd realised Kitty had turned into such a beauty while I was away, I'd certainly have come back sooner. You're a lucky devil, Julian, and I don't hesitate to say so in front of Kitty, since she's thoroughly spoilt already."

Kitty raised her head to smile up at him, and Julian turned to greet Celia, who he thought was looking worried about something. She smoothed away her frown as soon as she was aware of his gaze and offered him the chair between her and Kitty, which had apparently been occupied previously by Nicky Lambert, for he raised an enquiring eyebrow at her. She paid no attention to him, however, and he was obliged to hunt up a fourth chair, which he placed on her other side.

She looked a little disconcerted when he sat down and grinned amiably at her. Julian wondered if Nicky had been attempting to set up a flirt with Celia and made a mental note to warn him to tread carefully if he had any such intention. Not that Celia would do anything so foolish as to succumb to Nicky's blandishments. But she might take him in dislike for the attempt, and that would be a pity. He thought Nicky and Celia would get along well enough if there were none of that nonsense to overcome. They had a great deal in common, after all, that neither was yet aware of.

Julian had always admired Celia Morland for her honesty, her calm courage, and her trusting nature. Nicky seldom gave any outward sign of possessing any of these qualities, but Julian knew they were there. Celia had a mind of her own, too. Julian supposed that, because she was a woman and not allowed to behave so extravagantly as Nicky could and still be taken seriously, she hid her intelligence behind self-control. It was difficult to discern any warmth behind that surface, but Kitty had assured him that Celia even wrote poetry, so he must give her the benefit of the doubt. Julian *had* seen her laugh on occasion, a free and unselfconscious laugh that indicated at the least a pleasant disposition.

Nonetheless, however much he admired Celia Morland, Julian could not keep his mind on her for very long in Kitty's presence—particularly when, as now, his betrothed was in a merry mood and insisted on drawing him into the conversation.

"Julian, dear, you aren't really put out with me for inviting the Proctors to the manor, are you? Do tell Nicky you are not. After all, just think how diverting it will be to see them after all these years."

Julian smiled and pressed her small hand gently. "How can I possibly answer that without making myself out to be the veriest coxcomb?"

"You could always skirt the issue," Nicky advised him, "by pointing out that none of us—Kitty excepted, of course—has ever seen the famous lovers, never mind seeing them *again*."

It did not escape Julian's notice that Celia was studying Kitty especially intently just then, as if waiting for her to reveal some secret only Celia knew she harboured. He had to smile at that. Kitty had no secrets because she was incapable of keeping any.

She had always been like that, even as a child. Julian had first come upon Kitty one summer day when she was picking blackberries in a remote corner of his estate. She had understood she was trespassing and knew who he was, yet made no attempt to conceal her ill-gotten pinaforefull of berries. She had been only eight at the time and Julian a self-important three-and-twenty, but she brazened it out. Indeed, she had pointed out to him that he was making a great piece of work of nothing, for if she did not pick his berries the birds would get them. She then offered him a grubby handful; and he had found himself, against his will and intention, caught in her spell.

After that, he had made a point of cultivating the acquaintance of the Morlands, whose modest acres lay between Hardwicke Manor and the cliffs above Lyme Bay. He found Randolph Morland a sensible man with a deep knowledge of the land, which Julian was quick to appreciate and learn from. He took a brotherly interest in young Harry also, but it was Kitty who brought out of Julian something he would not have expected of himself—a gentler, kinder side of his nature. Although he did not realise it until years later, those qualities made him a better and more respected master of his lands and landlord to his tenants, as well as a more tolerant man towards both his servants and his peers. She made of him, in short, a gentleman.

Meanwhile, he had been aware that to Kitty he was something of a Prince Charming. He was flattered that even a child should see him in this light and careful not to disillusion her, for Kitty's good opinion was important to him. He even encouraged her by spinning tales, both true and fanciful, about the history of Dorset in general and the Hardwickes in particular. He gave her books to read, and she developed an especial fascination with mediaeval times. He described in imaginative detail life in the castles of that remote age, even rashly promising her one of her own to live in when she grew up.

He never believed that Kitty took any of this nonsense to heart. Surely, she was her father's child and knew the difference between childish fantasy and adult reality. When she was sent away to school in Bath, Julian put his mind to other things and forgot the fairy tales he had no further use for. Kitty, however, never forgot. At eighteen she returned home a radiant beauty, modishly gowned and coiffed and trailing a string of beaux. Before she had been back a day she came up to the manor and boldly demanded to see Julian, who by then had been lord of the manor for the three years since his father's death.

"You did not come for me," she accused him without preamble.

"I beg your pardon?"

Julian, understandably bemused, could only stare at this vision before him. He barely recognised the hoyden who had once upon a time, very long ago, invaded his blackberry patch. "Fetch you from the posting house, do you mean? I did offer, in fact, but Harry said he and Celia would meet you. Haven't they told you we're all to dine together here tonight?"

Kitty waited patiently for him to stumble to a halt. It struck him that she was very determined on something, but he could not imagine what it might be and waited with lively curiosity to find out.

"That is not what I mean," she told him in the manner of one explaining the most elementary lesson to a thick-headed pupil. Then her voice quavered a little, and for a moment Julian thought she was going to cry. "Oh, Julian, don't you remember at all?"

She had been holding a picturesque attitude before him, as if to show off her new bonnet and pelisse and grown-up figure. Then she flung away her muff and clutched at his sleeve, looking up at him from those devastatingly guileless blue eyes.

"You called me your fairy princess once," she reminded him. "You said you would come for me when I was grown up and—and would marry me and give me a castle to live in."

It came back to Julian then how Kitty had rebelled against being sent away to school. On the very day of her intended departure she had locked herself in her room and refused to set foot outside it ever again. Randolph Morland had sent for Julian, hoping he could prevent a fit of hysterics and coax Kitty into the chaise he had obligingly lent for the journey. She could then go off to be schooled—which in Kitty's loving, though exasperated, father's opinion was not only much needed but, since already paid for, should not go to waste.

Julian's persuasions had indeed succeeded in Kitty's departing quietly, even dry-eyed, although he distinctly remembered her watching out the window of the chaise until she could no longer see him waving after her. What he *had* forgotten was whatever Canterbury tale he had spun to achieve his objective. Years later, looking at that undeniably grown-up Kitty, stories began to emerge from his memory—of Cinderella and fairy princesses who waited patiently for their gallant knights to rescue them from their imprisonment by cruel guardians. He smiled at her and searched his mind for some way to apologise for his unscrupulous, though harmlessly intended, methods of persuasion, but Kitty would hear none of this.

"Well?" she demanded, stepping back and fixing him with a look that said she would accept no childish sops to her vanity this time. "Where is my castle?"

"Dear girl, surely you don't still—"

"You did not come for me," she informed him, "so I have come to you."

He searched her face for some sign that she was teasing him, but could see only earnest, even desperate, hope in her candid gaze. A notion flickered across his own mind that perhaps fairy tales did sometimes come true—that it was possible Kitty really did want him.

Before he could think better of such an absurd notion, he said, "I have only Hardwicke Manor, my dear. Is that castle enough for you?"

What happened after that was something Julian still sometimes thought must have been a dream and which he never spoke of even to Kitty for fear of its vanishing like some midnight fantasy in the light of day. His head remained level enough, however, not to give in to Kitty's wish to be married at once. She was too young, he said, though realising it untrue, to know her own mind. Besides, the county would be disappointed if he and Kitty did not make a proper celebration of their wedding and invite everyone they knew, and that would take time to arrange.

Surprisingly, Kitty did not object to the delay even when it stretched from six months to a year and then to after Kitty's twentieth birthday. Julian did not know why Kitty acquiesced in these delays, for he did not dare to try to explain to her the reasons behind them. She would only laugh at his premonition that something would happen to separate them and it was better that something should occur before they were married than afterwards. Still, now that what he had dreaded was indeed coming to pass, Julian could take no comfort in saying he had expected it all along.

It had begun long before Kitty informed him of the impending arrival of Sir Phineas and Lady Proctor, which seemed to Julian merely to set the final seal on the inevitable. The present Lady Proctor's relation to Julian's father had come to its ignoble end well before Julian's birth, and he had never met Lavinia. Nonetheless, he was well acquainted with the effect the affair had on his father from accounts by friends of how different the aloof, self-centred old man had been as a youth and even during his first marriage. What was more, Julian knew that Lavinia had run away precisely on the night after her twentieth birthday celebration. Superstition or not, Julian was taking no chances that history might repeat itself.

Yet, even this possibility paled beside Julian's more recent discovery among his father's papers of a dairy for the last year of James Hardwicke's first marriage. It made note, on a certain day in August 1777, that Lavinia was with child. Thus far, however, Julian had found no subsequent record of a birth, and his search was taking on a desperate urgency. Of all the possible consequences of Lavinia's pregnancy, the one becoming fixed in his mind as inevitable was that there had been a child and that child was a son—Julian's older half brother, the true heir to Hardwicke Manor.

For Julian himself, the existence of such a son would be devastating but not fatal. He had come to believe, however, that Kitty would be unwilling to marry him without his "castle." It was his own fault, of course, not only for filling her head full of nonsense about the manor when she was a child, but for making such a fuss over it since their engagement. He had ordered in glaziers and plasterers to make repairs, upholsterers and drapers to refurbish the main salons, and urged Kitty herself to decide what she might like to have done. He had become obsessed with details. He must have only the finest crystal for the chandeliers in the ballroom and only precisely the right shade of green for the dining room would do for him—because it was for her. Now he was reaping the results of his folly.

Julian had likewise convinced himself that locating Lavinia's missing son would put him out of his misery one way or another. Now he was torn between putting an end to his betrothal as quickly and mercifully as possible or maintaining the fiction of it for as long as he could. On the one hand, he did not know how long Kitty would continue to accept these delays in their wedding plans, and on the other he longed for some outside force to relieve him of his wretched indecision. He therefore both looked forward to and dreaded the arrival of Lavinia and her new husband.

"I should have liked to go to the royal wedding," Kitty sighed as she leafed through the account of the Princess Charlotte's recent nuptials in the Exeter newspaper Mr. Lambert had brought with him.

The four friends, having enjoyed one of the Hardwicke chef's exquisite meals, were sitting at their ease in Kitty's favourite drawing room. Julian preferred dark, discreet panelling and substantial furnishings. Kitty, however, had taken one look at the white walls, gilt trim, and pale green carpet in this room, and begged Julian not to change an inch of it. She declared it her future "audience chamber." She even made it a point to wear something pale green when she intended to sit in the room. Tonight that was a pair of delicate morocco slippers, which gave Julian a chance to admire her ankles.

"I would have taken you," he said, moving his eyes up her fine cambric gown to the pearl earbobs just visible behind the single curl that hung down her cheek. "But as I recall, you said at the time of their betrothal that both Charlotte and Leopold looked so solemn in the portraits that the wedding was unlikely to be amusing."

He smiled, less at the memory than at the realisation that Kitty was fully aware of his scrutiny. Little flirt.

"Oh, well, I daresay we should not have seen the bride and groom in any case," Kitty said, carelessly disregarding her future husband's probable influence at court. "But do look at these gowns the bridesmaids wore, Celia," she went on, passing a page of newsprint to her sister-in-law. "Would they have been all in white, do you suppose, or silver like the princess? And is that Valenciennes lace on the hems?

The princess had shells and flowers embroidered on her dress, but these don't look anything like that."

The gentlemen exchanged speaking glances. Kitty, although she did not look up from her illustrated newspaper, intercepted them and said, "You need not look, both of you, as if you wish you had stayed at the table for another glass of port. We are not going to talk about my trousseau. Anyway, Celia finds clothes quite as boring as you do."

Celia was moved to protest. "Why, Kitty, how you make me sound. I trust I do not look as if I give no thought to what I put on my back."

Kitty hastened to apologise for her mode of expression, but Celia only laughed and said she was teasing. Mr. Lambert looked Mrs. Morland over as if he would say something about her elegant green wool gown to contradict Kitty's gaucherie, but Julian was relieved when he did not. Celia was not immune to compliments, but she knew when she was being patronised. Anything Nicky might say then would be bound to sound just that. Nicky seemed to realise this as well and remarked instead to Kitty, who was too complacent to take any remark amiss, that Julian was fortunate to be getting a wife who knew when *not* to talk about some things.

"Julian has never learned to trust his good fortune," Kitty responded, "but I am teaching him."

"How very self-centred you are, Kitty," Nicky said indulgently. He had taken the most comfortable chair and put his elegantly shod feet up on a sturdy ottoman. He could afford, Julian thought, to be avuncular. "You are implying that you yourself are the good fortune that Julian must learn to appreciate."

"I implied no such thing," Kitty objected, but on consideration added, "Not that it isn't true, but *I* would not have said it."

Even Julian had to laugh at that as Nicky pursued the jest. "Most ladies would think it without saying it. They believe that because the object of their love is central to their existence, his existence must depend on theirs also.

Nevertheless, they are very jealous of their love and give it only sparingly."

"What nonsense!" Kitty told him roundly. "That is not jealousy, but romance. Ladies will give all their love where it is accepted, but gentlemen are so often embarrassed by being made the object of a whole-hearted and determined love that they unwittingly hurt us by refusing even a part of it."

"You ladies hedge your love with so many conditions and demands for proofs of exclusivity that it is no wonder that we hesitate."

"Exclusivity? When it is you gentlemen who insist on that, not trusting us to know our own minds? Worse yet, you consider loyalty to be only on one side. We wait only to be certain. For us exclusivity is beside the point and so should be on both sides."

"I rest my case. It is gentlemen who are the true romantics."

"But how can you say so?"

"Because they know what they want as soon as they see it and never change their minds. Ladies are natural flirts and dissipate their affection by giving away pieces of it willy-nilly while they wait for their little proofs. Am I not right, Julian?"

Nicky glanced at his host for confirmation, but Julian shook his head. "Oh, no. You will not draw me into this dispute. Whatever my own feelings, I dare not disagree with my bride-to-be in matters of the heart."

Nicky laughed. "Craven! But what about you, Mrs. Morland? Are you silent because you disagree with your own sex, or do you concur with Kitty that we are all fools about love?"

"I think we are all fools about it at one time or another," Celia said, "however briefly and unwillingly we may afterward admit to having been foolish."

Mr. Lambert put his feet back on the floor and leaned forward as if to reply to this possibly interesting confession, but they were never to hear of any lapse the sensible Mrs. Morland may have suffered into folly.

At that moment Jeffreys, Julian's stately butler, entered the room to announce, with something less than his customary sangfroid, "Sir Phineas and Lady Proctor have arrived, sir."

There was a moment's stunned silence before Mr. Lambert exclaimed, "Good God! Weren't they expected in the morning? What do you suppose brings them here in the middle of the night?"

"Oh, do hush, Nicky," Kitty admonished him. "They'll hear."

"Show them in, Jeffreys," Julian said, bracing himself.

Four pairs of curious eyes turned to the doorway, but for a moment there was only an indistinct, peevish murmur to be heard. Then Jeffreys flung the door open, and four faces revealed a common astonishment in four separate ways.

Julian's first impression of Lady Proctor—his stepmother, he supposed he might call her—was of her diminutive stature and only secondarily of her theatrical style of dress. As if she were aware that she had lost her good looks some years before, Lavinia attempted to make up with artifice what she lacked in nature. Her girlish coiffure was of an unnaturally bright scarlet, and when she removed her green satin roquelaure it was only to reveal an even more garish turquoise gown beneath. A large topaz pendant hung around her neck, and her fingers were bedecked with yet more colourful, although probably less valuable, stones set in heavy gold rings.

Indeed, she closely resembled a character in a farce Julian had seen the previous year in London. He suppressed his smile, schooled his expression to the blandness of the dutiful host, and stepped forward to welcome Lady Proctor, bowing over her beringed hand. She smiled then, and he caught a glimpse in her rouged, wrinkled face of the beauty she must once have been.

"Oh, you are Julian!" she exclaimed in a breathless, almost frightened voice. "I do beg your pardon most sincerely for intruding on you at such an unconscionable hour, but you see, Phineas was—that is, we found the inn at Lyme Regis dreadfully uncomfortable and would have been obliged to leave in the morning in any case, only—"

"Damp sheets!" boomed a deep voice behind her. "Couldn't have got a decent night's sleep there. Trust you don't mind putting us up tonight, eh, Hardwicke?"

Sir Phineas rolled into the room in his wife's wake, rumbling like thunder over Lyme Bay on a summer night. Julian thought he had never seen such a large man who was not actually fat. Sir Phineas was well over six feet tall and broad in proportion, resembling nothing so much as a large bulldog on which a decided turn for dandyism could only appear ridiculous. He was not unhandsome of feature, but his grey hair had receded to somewhere just above his ears and his large nose was very red—whether from the night air or the brandy bottle Julian dared not speculate. He coughed loudly, begged pardon, and held out one exquisitely manicured hand, which he took back again after the most perfunctory of handshakes.

"Of course I am delighted that you decided to come to me rather than be uncomfortable, sir," Julian assured him. "I daresay your rooms are already made up and need only to have the fires lit in them to be just what you would prefer. Won't you sit down for a moment before retiring and take some refreshment? Lady Proctor, a glass of ratafia, perhaps? And a brandy for you, Sir Phineas?"

Jeffreys, who had been hovering in the door, took the hint and removed himself to attend to rooms and refreshments while Julian turned back towards his dinner companions to present them formally.

It was then that he nearly gave into his initial ignoble impulse to laugh. Each one of the three was standing in precisely the same attitude he or she had assumed when the Proctors entered the room. They looked, Julian thought with a gleam of detached amusement in his eyes, like a parliament of stuffed owls.

3

SHE HAS NEVER seen them before in her life! was Celia's first thought.

Aware that her own gaze had been rudely fixed on the extraordinary couple who had just entered the room, she had looked away, intending to convey somehow to Kitty that they must take Julian's lead and welcome their guests in a manner more closely resembling customary Hardwicke hospitality. Then Celia caught Kitty's astonished look and realised at once that the Proctors were as much strangers to her as to everyone else. Why on earth had she pretended otherwise?

Happily, Julian was able to perform the introductions with nary a missed beat. Celia felt Sir Phineas's warm hand take hers firmly as he bent to greet her with a slight creak indicative of a corset beneath his very modish blue super-fine coat and striped silk waistcoat. She was able to look up at him then with a friendly smile on her lips and to greet Lady Proctor with a light kiss on her dry cheek, from which Celia came away enveloped in lavender scent and a dusting of rice powder.

Lady Proctor moved on to Kitty, who had by then altered her expression to one less revealing of her emotions and said with her natural unaffected warmth, "I'm so glad you were able to accept my invitation, ma'am."

Lavinia's expression was blank for a moment, then changed into a picture of vague good will as if—failing to recollect immediately the name of the person to whom she had just been introduced—she was attempting to pretend otherwise until someone else dropped the lost name into the conversation.

"Thank you so much, my love," she said, glancing about the room and fluttering her lacy handkerchief to indicate her general admiration of her new surroundings. "It is delightful to be here at last."

Kitty looked decidedly relieved at Lavinia's careful choice of words and gave her an especially warm embrace before leading her off to the sofa to engage her in conversation. Celia thought she understood the mystery now and was sufficiently glad there was nothing so very dreadful behind it that she was able to smile cordially at Nicholas Lambert, who caught her eye just at that moment. He made a step in her direction, which Celia countered by moving away to occupy the lone straight-backed chair next to the sofa.

When Jeffreys presently appeared with the brandy, followed by one of the footmen with a tray of cordials for the ladies, she took the tray and had begun to pour before looking up to see that Mr. Lambert had taken the matching chair opposite her own and was observing her with an amused gleam in his eye.

"I trust you had a comfortable journey into Dorset, sir," Julian said to Sir Phineas, who had turned himself so that he was facing the full-length portrait of Julian's grandfather on the wall behind him rather than looking directly at Julian.

"Beg pardon, my boy!" he shouted. "Left ear's gotten a bit troublesome, you know. It don't want to hear anything clearly."

Julian offered Sir Phineas a seat that positioned him more comfortably for conversation. He seized the opportunity to complain rumblingly about the distance from London which, although it had been covered in easy stages and the Proctors had a day's rest in Lyme Regis before proceeding to Hardwicke Manor, was still claiming its effect on Sir Phineas's never-robust constitution. Julian maintained a diplomatically sober countenance at this, but solicitously offered the remarkably robust-looking old knight yet another seat in the large, overstuffed armchair near the fire. Sir Phineas, however, declined to move his old bones once again.

Amidst Julian's diplomatic skills, Kitty's delight at playing lady of the manor, and Mr. Lambert's attentions being distracted by Lady Proctor, Celia was able to remain silent and observe the company in her usual contemplative fashion.

She was hard put not to smile at Lady Proctor, however, who was simpering coquettishly at Mr. Lambert and asking him if he were related to Martin Lambert, who had once—many years ago, to be sure—been a beau of hers. Nicky replied with a straight face that she must refer to his uncle, who had always had an eye for the ladies, especially the pretty ones. Lady Proctor lowered her remarkably black lashes at that and thanked him demurely.

Celia tried to detect the resemblance between this Lady Proctor and the young woman in the portrait upstairs, but in feature there seemed to be none. In her demure, but at the same time eager, expression, however, Celia imagined she could see a connexion, as if forty years had not changed Lady Proctor's character in any way. Yet she must be different now, having survived a notoriety that the young bride could not have imagined. If nothing else, she must feel some awkwardness at being obliged to carry on small talk in the very room where she must once have presided over the same sort of gathering. Celia tried to see herself in such a situation, but her imagination balked at it. In any case, she was not the sort of woman for whom men risked loss of pride and reputation, so she was scarcely likely to come to such an end.

Womanly curiosity, however, made her glance at Lady Proctor again to see what it was that could inspire such emotions. However, Lady Proctor's back was to her now, and Celia found Nicky Lambert's eyes on her instead. He winked impudently over Lady Proctor's red head, and Celia turned her look as steadily as she could to Julian, who was listening with every appearance of interest to Sir Phineas's description of their summer cottage in the northern mountains of India.

Celia had always admired Julian's ability to be equally gracious to every person who came to his notice. If this sometimes seemed to exclude those who were due a greater attention, Celia reminded herself that she did not know Julian well enough to fall within the small circle of his intimates and that she ought not therefore to judge him. She should, rather, learn by his example. In his skilled hands and lulled by his soft, deep voice, which was accustomed to flatter without appearing to fawn, both Proctors visibly mellowed. Within a very short time they appeared to be quite at home, even to the extent that Sir Phineas felt free to help himself to a second brandy before the hovering butler had divined that he wanted it.

"Allow me, sir," Jeffreys interrupted, taking the decanter from Sir Phineas's large grip and pouring a generous measure.

Sir Phineas's high shirt points prevented him from turning his head sufficiently to thank Jeffreys directly, but he waved his plump hand at the butler in a practised gesture that Celia guessed had been developed to deal with servants whose native language was foreign to him. There was nothing of the lordly nabob in his attitude, however, and Celia began to suspect that Sir Phineas might just be more amiable than his booming voice and overwhelming size at first gave one to assume.

"Well, Hardwicke," Sir Phineas boomed, "fine place you have here! Might even fancy such a house myself were I to seek one in the country, which I would not. Only drawback—a bit remote, ain't it?"

"Not so much as Calcutta or Bombay, sir."

Sir Phineas laughed at that in an even more penetrating way that brought all other conversations in the room to a temporary halt while he recovered from the joke.

"Right enough you are, young man! You needn't add that it's time we made our peace with our neighbours and settled once again on our native shores. Although I daresay a settlement somewhat more removed from the actual shore would suit us better. Terrible damps in this part of the country, ain't there?"

"It is often so in the spring," Julian said. "But we do not stint on fires at the manor. I'm sure you will be perfectly comfortable."

"Very old house, too, ain't it?" Sir Phineas went on. "Always belonged to your family, has it?"

"Only since the seventeenth century," Julian replied. "Parts of the manor go back to the Normans. It was moated once, but the lake west of the house is all that remains of that era."

"That'll account for the damp," Sir Phineas said with a perverse kind of satisfaction.

Julian agreed resignedly and settled back to endure further variations on what seemed to be Sir Phineas's favoured theme. Celia, disappointed that her shameless eavesdropping had yielded no confirmation of the Proctors' motives in coming to Hardwicke Manor, turned her attention to Kitty. She had been unable to persuade Mr. Lambert to remove to the sofa beside her when Lady Proctor deserted her to sit beside her husband and listen to the end of a rather drawn-out tale about a tiger hunt. Kitty sat now on the floor next to Mr. Lambert's chair, with her flower-trimmed skirts spread around her and her stiff pink satin stomacher obliging her to bend towards him with the mechanical, but oddly appealing movement of a clockwork doll.

He had perforce been obliged to join her on the carpet, and they now had their heads together like two children exchanging whispered confidences. Kitty was saying something to Mr. Lambert in a low but animated voice. He listened intently but with a slight air of detachment, until Kitty came to a halt and looked at him for confirmation of whatever it was she had told him. He gazed back at her then and smiled, and Celia felt another of those unaccountable and uncomfortable pangs of envy.

Her discomfort, however, was nothing compared to the shock of the wide-eyed look Kitty levelled at Nicky Lambert. It seemed to Celia to convey no less than unalloyed adoration and made clear to anyone who cared to look that Kitty was in love with Nicholas Lambert. To be sure, this ought not to be so surprising. Indeed, Celia told herself, it was a natural reaction on the part of a pretty young girl to be attracted to such a handsome and charming young man.

Suddenly, Celia understood Kitty's real reason for inviting the Proctors, sight unseen. She had meant to demonstrate to Nicky that a runaway romance such as theirs could have a happy ending.

For the first time, Celia was glad that the Proctors had proved so unromantic a pair. However, if such had indeed been Kitty's motive for inviting them, she must now begin again to court Nicky. Hence, the whispering.

But no! Surely Celia was letting her imagination run away with her. Kitty could not be so disloyal to her betrothed in his own home. Julian was still engaged in a somewhat one-sided conversation with Sir Phineas, and a look of polite ennui had settled upon his countenance. His mind was obviously miles away from the library. He was not even aware of Kitty's presence, much less of her behaviour.

Celia made a decision and, before she could change her mind about meddling, took it to Kitty. Mr. Lambert scrambled to his feet at her approach, but Celia disregarded him and knelt down beside Kitty, who smiled ingenuously and invited her to join them.

"Kitty, dear," Celia said in a low voice, "perhaps you ought to go and see if Mrs. Milsom needs any help with getting rooms ready for the Proctors."

"Oh, no," Kitty said, unconcerned. "Mrs. Milsom always knows what to do, and I am sure I will only be in the way. She is the housekeeper, you will remember," she explained to Mr. Lambert. "A most wonderful housekeeper, but she does put me in a quake sometimes. I can't think how I could possibly be of help to her, Celia."

"Well, then," Celia persisted, "perhaps you should show her that you take an interest. Servants expect the mistress to supervise their work even if you need not contribute to it, and you will soon be the mistress here, will you not?"

Kitty looked decidedly uncomfortable. Celia knew that this was neither the time nor the place to remind her of her responsibilities, but she was in no mood to indulge the girl.

"Celia, you go," Kitty said brightly, as if that were the obvious solution. "Mrs. Milsom respects you, and you will know what to do and say if anything has been overlooked."

"But, Kitty—" Celia caught Mr. Lambert's quizzical gaze upon her and, not wanting to seem to be lecturing Kitty, gave in. "Very well. But do at least tell Lady Proctor that she will be able to retire shortly. She looks a little tired, I think."

"Oh, yes, of course!" Kitty exclaimed, relief almost palpable in her expression. "I can do that. Will you come with me, Nicky?"

Mr. Lambert smiled but shook his head, and Kitty did not press him. Celia too went off to do her duty, with the distinct impression that Mr. Lambert was still watching her—whether censoriously or with sympathy, she could not care at that moment—as she made her excuses and left the room to seek out the housekeeper.

Mrs. Milsom, it transpired, was more in need of someone to complain to about the upset in her orderly household than of any assistance in putting it to rights.

"Those servants of theirs!" she exclaimed, glancing about to be sure they were not overheard as she bustled down the hall, Celia following behind. "His man is an Hindu or a Sikh or some such strange race, and he went straight down to the kitchen to announce that he would prepare his own meals, thank you very much—as if Cook's mutton wasn't good enough for him—and what's more, that he would eat them in his master's chamber, as he calls the west guest bedroom. Of all the heathenish notions."

"Well, we all of us fall into habits that must seem very odd to outsiders," Celia said, remembering the suit of armour and the large refectory table that decorated the bedroom in question and wondering what the Indian would make of those. Her remark fell on deaf ears.

"And milady's dresser," the housekeeper went on. "A gypsy, that's what she is, and I don't mean just that she's travelled about a good deal. Calls herself Signora di Lambrusco, if you can imagine that, but she's no more an Italian lady than I'm your Uncle Silas. Goes about muttering to herself, and Molly says that whatever language she talks sounds like rude language."

Celia made soothing noises as she assisted Mrs. Milsom in her duties, understanding from the housekeeper's lapses in grammar that they scarcely made an impression. They certainly did nothing to smooth her own conflicting emotions which, when she returned half an hour later to the drawing room, reassembled themselves into irritation at Julian, who gave every appearance of having been engaged since she left in the very same conversation with Sir Phineas. How, Celia demanded of herself, could Kitty not be attracted to the likes of Nicholas Lambert when the man who professed to love her—though Celia could not picture Julian professing anything of the sort—made no effort to provide the kind of attention he must know Kitty craved?

Now she thought of it, indeed, it seemed to Celia that Julian had always gone out of his way to picture life at Hardwicke Manor as ordinary, even dull—almost as if he really had no strong feeling for Kitty and was trying to supply her with reasons to break off the engagement: something which he, as a gentleman, would be only too aware he could not do. It was more likely, of course, that he simply wanted to forestall any disappointment Kitty might feel after their marriage at being shut away with little to do in a large, gloomy house whose management she had no interest in.

Still, this was certainly no way to woo her. Even Harry, Celia recalled with a little smile, had lied cheerfully to her about the delights of living with him in a tiny cottage with no servants but a daily housekeeper. Of course, Celia had been sensible enough even in the throes of courtship to know what was in store for her and had judged it worth the small discomforts. She could not be certain that Kitty was that clear-eyed.

Celia considered interrupting Sir Phineas's monologue and steering Julian in the direction of his wayward ladylove, but before she could decide on a subtle means to accomplish this, Jeffreys once again came to the rescue with the tea tray.

"Good heavens, is it ten o'clock already?" Kitty exclaimed, getting up from her schoolgirlish position with her leg crossed under her on the sofa and looking, Celia thought critically, a little flushed.

Celia was feeling critical of just about everyone at this point, and when Mr. Lambert rose gracefully to his feet and smiled at her, she scowled back. He kept his smile but raised his hands in a feinting gesture and took a step backwards as if fending off an attack. Celia lifted her chin and looked away.

"Oh, look, Julian, clotted cream!" Kitty exclaimed, taking the tray from Jeffreys and setting it down on a table near Lady Proctor. "You see, ma'am, what an honoured guest you are. We would not be allowed such a treat were it only Julian and I. Everyone here at the manor"—and here she sent Celia a speaking glance—"believes I am dreadfully spoiled, but I do so love cream on my cake, don't you? And here are some of Cook's delicious cakes."

Lavinia, thus encouraged, accepted a glass of sherry and a large dollop of cream on a piece of currant cake with every indication of delight. Celia's mood lightened somewhat, her irritation being transferred to herself for doubting Kitty's good sense. Here she was, after all, being properly attentive not only to Julian but to his guests. Celia even smiled when, having been served first by Kitty, Nicky immediately passed the plate on to Celia with a little bow. Somewhat molified, she deigned to exchange a few inanities with him as Kitty returned to Julian's side.

Unfortunately, Julian was not wise enough to make use

of this opportunity. Instead of drawing Kitty into a tête-à-tête that would leave her to retire to her bed with her mind filled with her betrothed and free from any influence Mr. Lambert might earlier have had on her, he manoeuvred her next to Sir Phineas and allowed the old knight to monopolise her attention while Julian devoted himself first to Lady Proctor, then to Mr. Lambert. Therefore, when the party broke up to repair to their rooms and Julian got around to saying a word to Celia, she found her irritation had returned.

It was difficult to be civil, much less sympathetic, when Julian remarked with a sigh, "Really, I cannot imagine what Kitty sees in them."

Celia had no doubt what he meant and replied unthinkingly, "Perhaps she is only looking for someone who will encourage her in her romantic notions."

This minor outburst did not make her feel any lighter of heart, however, and she removed herself from the room before any further unseemly remonstrance could escape.

Behind her, Julian and Nicky Lambert exchanged glances. Mr. Lambert raised an eyebrow inquiringly, and Mr. Hardwicke shook his head.

4

CELIA AWOKE EARLY the next morning despite the dissipations of the previous evening. She threw on a cloak over her old blue merino morning dress to take an early walk on the cliffs. She was a country girl, accustomed to walking. She had long ago discovered that the exercise alone was beneficial for clearing her mind of nonsense or worry and cheering her up as well.

So she set off briskly, covering the ground to the edge of the cliffs with long strides that woke her fully and blew the cobwebs out of her mind. Soon the bluster of the early hour wore off, and she was able to moderate her pace and loosen the cloak a little after the first mists had burned away and the blue of the sky deepened. There was still a sharp breeze, however, and Celia looked out instinctively towards the sea's horizon.

It was just such a day that Harry had liked best to sail—clear and brisk. He would go to the window directly upon awakening to look at the sky, and Celia always knew, when he turned back to her with that eager expression on his face, that he would gulp down the hastiest of breakfasts and be away before she had scarcely rubbed the sleep out of her eyes. Later, she would go out to the cliffs to search for his sail and she would wave, even knowing he would probably not see her.

She stopped now, just at the spot she had last seen him. There was another sail on the water today, an unfamiliar one. She waved just the same, and to her delight someone on the boat waved a bright yellow handkerchief back at her. She laughed.

It no longer pained her to remember Harry, although the last time she saw him from this cliff had been the day he died. She had stood there, watching the storm clouds she warned him about earlier grow larger and blacker. He had been showing off, performing intricate manoeuvres with the sail to make the little boat seem literally to dance on the waves, and she could only hope his skill would keep him upright on them.

It had not. Celia watched helplessly as a mass of angry cloud detached itself from the solid grey on the horizon, then scooped up water from the sea as it raced towards Harry's boat, which appeared to grow smaller as the squall grew larger and more fierce. Celia saw it happen, but was unable to stop it, from where she stood. The squall engulfed the boat like the whale swallowing Jonah. She had peered into the mist that was quickly condensing into rain but could see nothing. Then she ran for help.

The same storm, having once tasted land, refused to let go and raged for two days. A rescue party tried to set out three times. On the last attempt, a man was washed overboard and drowned and they gave up. It was not until a week later that Harry's body was found washed up on the beach two miles south of the spot where Celia now stood.

She had never been so foolish as to suppose that her cautious admonitions had spurred Harry on to greater risks than he would have otherwise taken that day. He was well accustomed to her caution, and she to his heedlessness. It had been an accident, pure and simple.

What had caused Celia more than one pang of guilt, however, had been her growing sense, even before Harry's death, that their marriage was a mistake. She had never been right for him, she knew. After his death her shameful relief that their marriage had ended early, while they were still happy together, only confirmed her first suspicion that their relationship was an aberration from the moment they met.

Kitty had been responsible for getting them together in the first place. The girls met at the Bath seminary where Celia was in her final year, having overcome by study and hard work the initial stigma of entering as an orphaned charity girl. She looked forward to teaching there herself in two more years and enjoying a respected position as well as, she hoped, the trust of all the other girls to come. When Kitty arrived, she looked so woebegone that Celia was reminded of herself at that age. She went out of her way to befriend the girl, little knowing that Kitty would be the first and last to whom she would serve as mentor and example.

All that immediately ailed Kitty, it turned out, was homesickness. By the time that had passed, she and Celia were firm friends, so that at the end of her first term Kitty had insisted on taking Celia home for Christmas. That was when she met Harry.

"Hullo!" had been his first word to her, accompanied, as so many of them later were, by a merry laugh. "Are you in the wrong house, or am I?"

To say that Celia was not absolutely certain of the answer was to confirm that she was considerably surprised to encounter him. Well, he *was* in the kitchen at three o'clock in the morning, she reminded Kitty later; but Kitty saw nothing extraordinary about that. Celia had been unable to sleep and tiptoed downstairs to make herself some hot milk. Harry had been out with some friends and was a little the worse for liquids other than milk. He had come in through the kitchen in order not to wake his mother and have to endure—he said—one of her thundering scolds.

Celia knew Mrs. Morland well enough by then to be aware that she never scolded her children—which, in her husband's opinion, accounted for a great deal of what was wrong with them. Celia smiled at Harry and shook her head, still not trusting herself to speak, much less to laugh.

"You don't believe me?" he said, "or you don't think I deserve a scold?"

"Oh, I'm sure you do," Celia answered solemnly, sending

Harry off into another peal of laughter which, if his mother had cared at all, would surely have brought her running. But it did not.

"So! I look as if I must have done something at some time in my ill-spent life to deserve a scold. Is that it?"

"Oh, no!—"

"Look here," he demanded. "Who *are* you, anyhow?"

The odd thing—one of the odd things—about Harry was that he behaved no differently the next day, when he had supposedly sobered up. He teased Celia about *her* having been caught prowling around the kitchen at a scandalous hour of the morning, as if she were the one who was at fault. She tried to hush him up, not wanting Mrs. Morland to know she had been unable to sleep. Thus Celia made herself appear guilty and delighted Harry no end.

Another odd thing was that Celia, who had up to then disliked intensely being teased, found herself enjoying it when it came from Harry. After a little while, she even learned to tease him back. She never became very adept at the practice, but it pleased Harry so that she became, without realising it, more like the Morlands all the time. She soon began to feel for the first time that she had a family of her own. After the girls went back to school, Harry began coming to visit them there, causing no end of consternation among the mistresses and excited giggles among the girls. Even Kitty was surprised, and Celia could not help feeling a little self-satisfied that this engaging young man— whom the more romantically-minded of the upper-form girls declared looked just like one of Byron's heroes—had most pointedly come to see her.

Harry, however, saw something different in the other girls' behaviour.

"They all admire you," he told her.

"Oh, no," Celia said, with a laugh at his lack of self-consciousness. "They envy me."

"Well, that as well, I suppose," he said, perfectly in earnest. "They wish they were more like you. One of the mistresses told me it's because you play no favourites, but treat them all justly and generously. An unusual combination, she said. Very desirable in a teacher."

They had stolen a few minutes to walk in the gardens behind the school building, and Harry stopped just then to look at her consideringly. After a moment he said, "Do you want to be a teacher?"

She didn't know what to say. Up to that moment teaching had been her highest ambition. Now, suddenly, she thought there might be something she would enjoy even more, but she did not dare voice the thought. Instead, she smiled, and said, "I think I have a great deal to learn first."

From that point on, the teasing turned quickly to flirtation and the laughter to words of love and at last, amidst Celia's disbelieving astonishment, to an offer of marriage which, at first, she refused.

"I see what it is," Harry said. "You believe I am beneath you. You will not lower yourself to marry a fribble who doesn't know the difference between Shakespeare and Sheridan, and for that matter—where did this stain on my coat come from, do you suppose? I made sure I was spotless before I came to see you—for that matter, one who is so clumsy he cannot even dress himself properly in the morning."

"Lower myself?"

Celia was so incensed that he would consider her above his touch that she did not even hear the rest of his nonsense. Otherwise, she would have told him that it was neither the quickness of his wit nor the weight of his learning that she respected—not that he had a great amount of either, and not very much ambition, besides. But she had never met anyone so graceful on a boat or a horse or a fast curricle or who made her laugh so often as he did. What did it matter that he had mud on his top boots?

"Harry, how can you be so—idiotish!" she said, stamping her foot in vexation at herself for even fleetingly harbouring a critical thought about him.

He looked up from his repentant little-boy posture then,

so that she could see the twinkle in his eyes, and she had laughed at being so taken in again. After he had asked her several more times to marry him, she had let her heart rule her head and had given in. Very soon after, she found herself married and living happily in the little cottage by the sea that the Morlands, who welcomed their new daughter with the same warmth Kitty and Harry showed her, had given them as a wedding present.

As she looked back on it now, Celia thought that the first shadow on their happiness had perhaps come when Harry's father and mother died within a year of each other. That set Harry to thinking somber thoughts about the future. After Kitty came to live with them, he took Celia aside one night and extracted a promise from her that if anything ever happened to him, she would look after Kitty.

"You could do it better than anyone, I know," he told her. "And in a way, you'll be a teacher to her after all, won't you?"

Celia had adjured him not to talk as if it were a settled thing, but she had already had her own intimations that something would happen, though not something so desperate as his dying. Even now she could not believe that their life together would have gone on in the carefree way it had begun. She had never doubted Harry's love, and she had enjoyed the freedom being married to him gave her— the freedom to behave precisely as she pleased, or rather as Harry pleased her to behave, which was the same thing, with no thought for the morrow.

After the accident, which had come on her as unexpectedly as Harry in the kitchen that night, and after Harry was buried in the little churchyard not far from their cottage, Celia retreated into herself. She was determined never to risk such an unnatural attachment again or any other relationship that was not with what she considered her own kind—the safe, bookish, unemotional person who might not make her laugh but would not make her cry either.

Kitty, of course, was convinced that Celia would become a recluse, refusing to marry again because that would spoil the memory of her first, perfect love. Celia had no intention of telling Kitty what she truly felt, but she did succeed in convincing her that the happiness she had shared with Harry made her more willing to wait for just the right offer.

Celia had supposed that Kitty felt a certain amount of remorse for having introduced her to Harry in the first place, but that notion vanished as quickly as it had flared when Celia realised that Kitty simply liked to meddle. In fact, she liked to meddle best when she was convinced she was in the right and everyone would agree with her as soon as she had shown them so.

"I understand, darling," Kitty therefore assured her, when Celia declined to meet yet another perfectly lovely young man. "When one has been so happy in love as you have, one cannot imagine ever being so again. But there is no need to be hasty. I daresay you will be quite as pretty at five-and-twenty as you are now and will have no end of suitors."

Celia was now almost four-and-twenty, and she could only hope that Kitty's own marriage would serve to distract her from her sister-in-law's advancing years and declining prospects. Meanwhile, there had been no surfeit of suitors—indeed, scarcely a sprinkling. Celia had been glad of that, since it cost her no heartache to turn any of them down. But there was no telling what schemes Kitty might hatch when she was finally settled herself.

Not that this prospect was as immediate as it had once seemed. Celia came just then upon an outcropping of rock that prevented her from continuing along the ridge in the direction she had been going. She turned her steps back the way she had come and her mind once again to the puzzle of why precisely Kitty had invited the Proctors to Hardwicke Manor and then lied about how she had done it. Was this fiction of having met them in Lyme Regis and extended an impulsive invitation intended merely to prevent a scold from Julian for imposing them on him? If so, that still did not explain why Kitty had extended the invitation, presumably by post, in the first place. Celia was reluctant to think that Kitty planned to emulate their example by eloping with Nicky Lambert, but it was the only explanation that made sense to her. Furthermore, while it might be a temporary setback that the elderly lovers turned out to be such an unattractive example, Celia could not be sure that this would deter Kitty, who obviously adored Nicky. And he must be entranced by her as well. What man would not be?

Celia's mind drifted briefly into contemplation of Kitty and Nicky happily raising a family of beautiful children in the midst of what she imagined must be a tropical paradise called Indigo Hill Plantation, Jamaica. Celia's romantic streak might be buried deeper, but it was as pronounced as Kitty's. On the other hand, Celia was all too well acquainted with the ease with which one could fall in love with charm, and Nicky Lambert was far too charming for anyone's good. Furthermore, although she supposed Julian would survive the setback, she did not want to see him or his pride hurt.

In the meantime, Julian had been not only gracious to the Proctors, but remarkably tolerant of the intrusion on his household. Their two carriageloads of baggage and their peculiar servants and habits were certainly more disruptive belowstairs than in the master's study. Nonetheless, Julian deserved much credit for making his guests welcome and tactfully ignoring—as least so far as Celia was aware—any mention of the past.

Celia had done her best to smooth the ruffled sensibilities of the kitchen and pantry servants without placing herself in a position that might be considered interfering. It was not her house, after all. However, since Kitty, whose house it soon would be, showed no inclination to take over its management any sooner than necessary, someone had to see that dinners were planned and prepared and that sheets were changed and picture frames dusted. Kitty's attitude of benign neglect was not one Celia understood. When she taxed Kitty with it, she only shrugged and said that Mrs. Milsom was perfectly capable and one did not want the servants to be bored, did one?

Celia smiled at the absurdity of this notion, but decided that instilling some sense of domestic responsibility into Kitty was a task for a schoolteacher, not a friend. She had taken Harry's request to heart and looked after Kitty as best she could, but best was not as a teacher, she had decided. A friend waited to be asked, no matter how tempting it might be to meddle, Kitty-fashion, in other people's lives.

The path dipped towards the valley to the seaward of the manor, and the house came into view again. Celia stopped for a moment and breathed deeply, taking the fragrant air into her lungs as her eyes absorbed the spectacular view of the estate. Her walk had accomplished what she set out to do. Now she felt able to face the day—including Indian valets and Italian maids and ruffled English sensibilities—calmly.

In the distance, a church clock chimed. Startled, Celia pulled out her pocket watch—Harry's watch, which was too big to wear around her neck so she kept it in her petticoat pocket. Good heavens, she had been roaming about for more than an hour! Everyone would be wondering what had become of her. Besides, the fresh air had made her ravenous. She set off on the last quarter mile at a quick walk, hoping there would be some breakfast left.

5

CELIA HAD OVERESTIMATED the stamina of the rest of the household. When she arrived slightly breathless back at the manor and entered the breakfast parlour, she found Mr. Lambert in sole possession, helping himself liberally from covered dishes of eggs, ham, and fish.

Breakfast was a haphazard meal at the manor, and at no time more so than when guests were in residence. It was Julian's policy that people ought to be able to begin the day at their own pace. The result was that even if one came down at the same hour every day, there was no telling whom one might encounter there. Celia did not really expect to see the Proctors at this hour, but she was a little surprised to find Mr. Lambert there, and without Kitty.

"Good morning, Mrs. Morland," he said, laying down his plate and pulling out a chair for her. When she moved to protest, he insisted on getting whatever she wanted to eat for her.

"You look as if you have been running, but I assure you there is plenty left. Even Julian isn't down yet—or is having his breakfast in the fastness of his study."

"Good morning, Mr. Lambert," she said, then felt obliged to explain after she had caught her breath, "I have not been running. I went out for a walk and lost track of the time, that is all. I did not want anyone to be concerned."

She stopped, realising how self-consequential that sounded. If no one was yet up, obviously no one would have missed her, much less been concerned. She gave up and submitted to being waited on in comfort. As usual, there was a dish from savoury to sweet to suit every taste. Celia knew that Jeffreys would appear as if by magic whenever the tea or coffee neared the bottom of the pot. The curtains had not yet been opened over the French windows which, in any case, gave onto the low hills to the south so that morning sunlight did not enter the room directly. The fire was still burning low, and the room proved an unexpectedly warm and pleasant antidote to her more-than-ample dose of fresh morning air.

Mr. Lambert deposited a plate of ham and shirred eggs garnished with slices of apple in front of her. Exactly what she would have chosen herself, she was disconcerted to observe.

"I saw you leave," he said in a confidential whisper, as if they were not alone in the room. Then, in a normal voice, he added, "I mentioned it to Jeffreys, and he said that you usually go walking before breakfast. So you see, you would have been missed, but not worried about."

He seated himself and poured coffee out for both of them. "An admirably healthful habit, I must say, morning walks. I am all envy, but I fear my energies are not up to your own at this early and very brisk hour."

"Yet here you are," she said.

He grinned. "I was hungry. If you look a little closer, you will discover me still unshaved and my neckcloth a mere approximation of gentlemanly style."

Since he had said it, Celia could not help looking, but the quirk in his cheek when he tried not to laugh made her pick up her fork and direct her eyes once again to her ham and eggs. She wished he were not so easy to look at. Even in semi-déshabillé, he appeared elegantly dressed. Despite the long nose and the high forehead, his was a distractingly handsome face above the immaculate linen shirt and grey silk waistcoat. She contrived not to look into those candid hazel eyes that were as ingenuous as a tidal pool, inviting one to fall in.

His shapely brows drew together slightly, as he asked, "How is it we have not met before, Mrs. Morland? I cannot imagine that I would have forgotten the occasion if we had."

"I only came to live in the district just before my marriage," Celia explained, "and as I believe you had then already been established for some time in Jamaica, it is not surprising that our paths did not cross. Before that I had lived in North Devon all my life. When you last visited your family, Harry and I were on our honeymoon. We went to Wales," she added, as if it mattered.

"Yes, I remember being sorry to miss him and sorry to miss meeting the new Mrs. Morland. Julian was full of praise of you."

He narrowed his eyes a little, as if trying to remember something, then added, *"Her voice, her touch, might give th'alarm; 'Twas both perhaps, or neither; In short, 'twas that provoking charm; Of Celia altogether."*

Celia had no difficulty imagining Julian's attitude towards her at the time of her marriage, and she knew that he would never have expressed it in Mr. Whitehead's words. At least she could depend on Julian's not quoting that particular poem either to or about her. She was a little disappointed that Mr. Lambert was not above what so many others mistakenly felt would impress her.

"I expect that what he said was that I should be a sobering influence on Harry," she said dryly, reminding herself that she should be grateful that no one ever thought to recite Ben Johnson's *Ode to Celia* to her.

He looked at her closely over the rim of his coffee cup. "Were you?"

She gave him a questioning look.

"Good for Harry," he reminded her.

"Oh. I'm afraid not. Harry was well established in his habits by then, and I could not have changed him even had I wished to."

"I thought all women married for the sole purpose of reforming their husbands."

She glanced at him quizzically. "I think you are saying that only to provoke me. You cannot believe it."

"You are very astute, ma'am. I expect you had Harry's

measure long before you married him."

She was not entirely sure what he meant by that, but she had no intention of embarking on a discussion of her marriage nor of defending herself against a charge of being the managing female he seemed to imply. She did not reply, therefore, instead picking up the coffee pot and offering to refill his cup, which he obediently held out to her.

He had finished his own breakfast and laid down his knife and fork. After a moment, however, it became apparent that he was not going to oblige her by taking up the conversation again. Celia cast about for some subject that did not tread on delicate ground.

"I take it that Sir Phineas and Lady Proctor have not yet been down to breakfast?" she asked.

"Not since I have been here. I have an unworthy suspicion that it takes both of them some hours to reconstruct themselves every morning. We may never see them at breakfast."

"You are unkind to imply you are glad of it."

"I imply nothing. Like Alceste in Molière's play, I am only being honest. Unlike him, however, I do not say such things to people's faces."

"Then like the hero of the same playwright's *Tartuffe*, you are a hypocrite, sir."

"So are we all to some extent, and of necessity. It oils the wheels of social intercourse to pretend amiability one does not feel, but it relieves one's frustration to be unamiable in private."

"If I were to repeat your remarks, your reputation for amiability would vanish like the insubstantial thing it is."

"But you would not do so."

"How do you know that?"

"Because you are an honest woman, and her price is above rubies."

"If you have been waiting to catch me out on one of these quotations you persist in throwing at me," she said, "you have failed. That one is incorrect."

He leaned back in his chair and smiled. "Kitty told me

you would have been a good schoolmistress. I see that she was right."

"There is more to it than a talent for the apt remark, you know."

"I imagine there must be," he said. "I had a tutor once who rarely opened a book and whose idea of learning was to travel abroad whenever he had the opportunity and—as he put it—observe the native life. He did bring back the most amazing artifacts from places we had never previously heard of, and we awaited his return each time as if he were Father Christmas. I suppose we did learn a good deal from him, even if it was of little use in passing entrance exams to university. Do you like to travel, Mrs. Morland?"

"I think I should like it, but I must confess to never having been farther from here than Holyhead."

"Not even to London?"

"I regret not. I do have an extensive corresponding acquaintance there, however, and they tell me of everything—the theatre and parties and so on. That is quite enough for me."

"That is not quite the same as seeing it all for yourself. Why don't you go?"

She smiled. "Just like that? It would hardly be proper. You forget that gentlemen may go where they please with no one commenting one way or the other, but we ladies are not so free."

"Nonsense. Even in England, ladies travel about visiting one another."

"Whom am I to visit?"

"Make one of your correspondents invite you."

"Oh, I don't think so," she said placidly, but with a smile at his naïveté. "In any case, I am perfectly content here."

"Doing what?"

"Chaperoning Kitty, mainly. I do a little gardening. I read a great deal."

"What a lively time of it you must have. What about when Kitty is married?"

"I shall go back to my own home."

"And do what?"

She glanced at him much as she would have at a recalcitrant pupil, hoping it might have the same effect. "Precisely what I have always done."

He smiled, acknowledging the hint. "Very well, I shall mind my own business, but I shall ferret out whatever it is you are keeping from me. Depend on it."

She did not doubt he meant it, and she did not really mind if he discovered from Kitty or Julian about her writing. She was, however, reluctant to discuss it when she knew him so little. He might, as strangers had done in the past, dissipate some of the feeling she had for her poetry by reducing it to polite small talk. True, he seemed sufficiently intelligent not to do that. Yet, even if he did prove a sympathetic listener, she would rather he read what she wrote so that she would not have to explain it.

"Tell me at least what you do for amusement here at the manor," he said. "Do you ride?"

"Not with any grace. I'm afraid I consider a horse to be simply a means of locomotion. Julian rarely gives me one of his prime bits, as Sam the groom calls them, to ride. Old Polly gets me where I am going, and that is all I ask."

"Remind me not to be seen in your equestrian company. I at least have a reputation to maintain."

"Oh, is that what your reputation rests on?" she asked innocently.

He laughed and leaned forward again to fix her with a look that had more than a hint of mischief behind it.

"Forgive me, but do you know, I still cannot recall it, although I have been searching my memory since the subject came up. What is the correct version of that quotation I misused earlier? I should not like to mistake it again."

"If you have forgotten it, sir, I suggest you consult your Bible—if you have one. You will find the quotation in Proverbs."

He laughed at that. "I have the distinct impression, Mrs. Morland, that you do not approve of me," he said.

"You are a trifler, sir," she said, mincing no words.

"I?" He sounded genuinely stunned. "Please tell me, ma'am, what I have done to earn such an unjust epithet. With whom have I trifled?"

Celia was sorry she had made the accusation, but having done so it was only fair to explain herself.

"You flirted with Kitty."

"I always do," was his unexpected reply. "It is a kind of game we play, scarcely to be considered trifling, since we both know the rules and play by them."

That set Celia properly in her place as one who did not know the rules. It was true enough. She had never been adept at the little games ladies and gentlemen played with each other in the name of courtship. She had been an only child with no brothers to instruct her in how to be at ease among gentlemen. She had spent her youth in the company of women and other girls of her age, and Harry had been her first and only admirer. Since she had never been quite sure what he had seen in her, she could not use whatever it was to her advantage now.

"Well, it is too bad of you to encourage Kitty. She may, despite your confidence in the rules of the game, take you in earnest."

"I do not encourage her," he said. When she responded with a skeptical look, he smiled and added, "I do not encourage anyone."

"You do not have to," Celia said, then could have bitten her tongue when he gave a shout of delighted laughter.

"What do you advise me to do, ma'am?" he asked, his mouth serious but his eyes dancing. "Will you exile me to the Indies again?"

"Considering your innocent or, at least, ingenuous charms, sir, that would perhaps be advisable. However, I would not wish to be the one to so advise you."

"What else is there to do, alas?"

"You should, perhaps, be more aware of your effect."

"I am learning rapidly, ma'am, that I seem to have no effect at all on *you*."

He watched her for a moment with interest as she searched her mind for a suitable rejoinder to this entirely unsuitable challenge. But when she did answer at last, she could almost predict the smile that said accusingly, *Aha! You cannot meet me on that ground, so you are changing the subject.*

"I understand we may expect an addition to the house party today," she said.

"Yet another pair of elderly eccentrics, I believe, by the name of Danby-Davis," he said, adding slyly, "or so Kitty describes them."

Celia had to smile. "For Kitty, that is a remarkable understatement. The last time we were privileged to receive them, they had just returned from a tour of South America where they had acquired some rather strange sort of tobacco, which they smoked in pipes after dinner. The next morning they would report the most fantastical dreams to us, which could not be wondered at, since the rest of us had felt quite giddy merely being in the same room as their pipes."

"I suspect it was one of the native opiates, which they would have obtained in Mexico or Peru."

"Yes, one of their tales was about an ancient priest in a village high in the Andes, although we gave no more credence to that than to any of their other stories. How do you know about it?"

"You underestimate me, Mrs. Morland," he said, putting down his empty cup and taking advantage of Julian's laissez-faire policy of hospitality by lifting his feet up on another chair.

"I do not merely occupy space in Jamaica, you know. I try to take an interest in everything that affects what is now my homeland. A good deal of the traffic in these substances flows through the island. Not all of it ends up in the hands of those whom it will not hurt, such as the Danby-Davises. In fact, that is why I came here three years ago—to read a report before the College of Physicians on the harm these narcotics do when dispensed too freely. Unfortunately, I was not taken seriously despite the evidence and case histories I presented. It requires more than one report to change the attitudes of people to whom such problems are unknown, who protest that their wives take laudanum for the headache and it does them no harm."

Celia did not speak immediately, wondering what extraordinary subject Mr. Lambert might prove expert in next.

"Well, Mrs. Morland, I perceive by your astounded silence that you do indeed consider me a trifler. Why should I not take an interest in serious matters?"

"I beg your pardon, I'm sure."

"Pardon is granted—on condition that you do not look quite so astonished in future if I should utter a word of beyond two syllables or voice an opinion on anything more substantial than the polish of my boots or the latest style in ladies' bonnets."

"Do you have an opinion on ladies' bonnets?" she could not resist asking.

"Only that they should be worn solely by women who need to hide their faces. You, I trust, do not even own one—at least, no more than one, and that for church. It would not do to be provocative in church as well."

She searched a moment in vain for a rejoinder before he laughed at her consternation and said, "It is as well you are an honest woman, ma'am, for you have the most expressive face I have ever encountered. You would be caught out in a lie at once."

"Happily I rarely find it necessary to dissemble, much less to lie."

"One must admire your self-control. Presumably that is what made Julian think you would be an influence for good on Kitty's brother."

"Thank you," she said, not knowing how else to respond to such an odd compliment.

Could he possibly believe that Julian Hardwicke's opinion was so important to her? It was not that she was indifferent, of course, but she and Julian had always respected each other without any particularly warm feeling on either side. Or could Mr. Lambert have been thinking? . . . Oh, surely not!

Startled by the notion, she looked up at him, only to find his hazel eyes once again alight with amusement.

"I must confess, however, that I admired you more when your self-control slipped a little," he said.

"When was that?"

"Last night, when you castigated Julian for being unromantic."

"I'm sure I did no such thing!"

"I beg to differ. You as much as told him that he should encourage Kitty in her notions."

"I only meant . . . Oh, dear." Celia remembered now precisely what she had said. "I shall have to apologise to Mr. Hardwicke. That was very uncivil of me."

"But true nonetheless."

"What do you mean?"

He studied her for a moment, then seemed to accept what her expression told him: that she really did not understand him. However, instead of explaining, he asked, "Why do you let Kitty take advantage of you so?"

Celia was beginning to be decidedly uncomfortable. How could he be so perceptive, yet so mysterious? He seemed to understand things about her that she did not know herself. She turned her face away from him, in case he could read there what she felt as well as what she thought.

"She made you do her work for her, by sending you to deal with the housekeeper," he continued. "Kitty is perfectly able to do that herself. You must not indulge her."

"She may be able to do so, but she does not care to. I do not mind. On the contrary, I enjoy it."

"So would Kitty if she could be persuaded that such tasks put her in a romantic light."

She would not ask him again to explain himself, Celia thought, and so said nothing. He laughed.

"What I mean, dear Mrs. Morland, is that Kitty is very conscious of how she appears to Julian and fears certain activities might spoil the pretty picture she presents of herself.

"But of course," he added, "being an honest woman, you

never suspected even Kitty of artifice of that kind."

Celia could feel herself blush again. Of course she had considered it, but how could she say so? Furious at him for putting her on the defensive like that, Celia stiffened her resolve not to let him charm her into any more indiscretions.

"You need not waste your wiles on me, Mr. Lambert. I can be of no possible use to you."

His tone sobered instantly, throwing her off her guard once more. "I beg your pardon, ma'am. I had no intention of insulting you. Certainly not by such means."

She stole a look at him and found him entirely in earnest, which inexplicably disappointed her. Surely she did not want him to go on teasing her in that disconcerting manner? Yet, how could he so quickly change from flirtatiousness to sobriety? Indeed, he could be both at once with no effort at all. Celia began to think that Nicky Lambert was a more dangerous influence than she had first given him credit for. If she could not resist being manipulated by him, what chance did poor Kitty have when she was so susceptible to flattery and in need of constant reassurance about her worth?

Fortunately, Celia was allowed a respite to consider this problem, as Julian joined them in the breakfast parlour bearing apologies from Kitty, who had overslept and was not hungry in any case. Feeling that she could therefore remove herself from Mr. Lambert's disconcerting presence with no fear of his spiriting Kitty away, Celia excused herself on the grounds that the gentlemen must have a good deal to talk about since they had not seen each other for so long.

However, once she had left the room, she had to lean back on the door for a moment to catch her breath.

6

KITTY HAD BEEN confident that the Proctors would find that they had much in common with the Danby-Davises. However, when Mr. Hardwicke's last guests arrived—on horseback and with, they assured their bemused host, no more baggage than a third horse could carry—they proved a contrast in every way to the nevertheless equally eccentric Proctors.

"A giraffe," was Mr. Lambert's sotto voce comment when he first laid eyes on Henrietta Danby-Davis.

Indeed, that lady did have not only a long neck but long, rather ungainly legs as well. They carried her everywhere at a determined though slightly awkward gait, only partially accounted for by her flowing garments that appeared to be an anglicised version of a desert Bedouin's robes. In colouring she was brown, except for her white hair; in age, somewhere indeterminate between forty and seventy; in disposition, almost relentlessly cheerful.

Her husband, Godfrey, was even taller and more angular. His clean-shaven face was so creased from exposure to the sun that—as Lavinia Proctor remarked over an afternoon game of quoits on the front lawn, which had been interrupted by the Danby-Davises who had declined to take part—he looked like nothing so much as an Indian fakir.

This elicited a rude noise from her husband, who added, more intelligibly, "Civil servants!" to which Lady Proctor nodded her agreement.

Mr. Lambert glanced at Mrs. Morland, who stood across the lawn from him, and smiled when he saw her eyebrows raised in unspoken censure of this remark. Meanwhile, Mr. Hardwicke was obliged to explain to his betrothed that the caste system in India to some extent spilled over into the lives of its English population. Consequently, she must not be very surprised if the Proctors appeared condescending to the Danby-Davises and the Danby-Davises appeared to toady to the Proctors.

"Or contrarywise," added Mr. Lambert, "considering the source of the Proctors' prosperity."

He tossed his quoit but missed the hob by several inches. Celia transferred her censure to him, since they were partnered, but tempered it with a light smile. She was well aware that her own skill at the game was of the slightest.

"Oh, but that's all nonsense," Kitty declared. "Anyway, those things don't matter here at the manor. I hope that I, for one, treat all of Julian's guests equally."

"Then I shall go home again," Mr. Lambert declared. "I cannot have you flirting with Godfrey Danby-Davis before my very eyes."

Everyone was relieved to discover that the Danby-Davises had given up inhaling noxious fumes and having fantastical visions as a result. Unfortunately, they had now gone off in an entirely new direction, acquiring such habits of healthy living as proved equally exasperating to the servants. It seemed the Danby-Davises could abide the ingestion of nothing that did not contribute to their greater physical well-being. Henrietta promptly sent a message to the kitchen that she required a pot of boiling hot water at breakfast to make her own infusions—which the cook would not dignify by the name of tea. And Godfrey somewhat condescendingly took Julian aside to explain that the port his father had laid down for special occasions was the fastest possible way to ruination of the liver.

"I suppose," said Julian over a late supper the next day long after the Danby-Davises had taken themselves off to their early, more healthful beds, "that when the pendulum swings back again it will be in progressively smaller arcs, and sooner or later they will behave quite normally."

Sir Phineas grunted as if this were a highly unlikely expectation. Kitty, who always tried to see the best in anyone, declared that she found the Danby-Davises amusing, to which Lady Proctor replied that standards of entertainment must be very lax in the country. Celia glanced at Julian, but he seemed to take no offence at this oblique aspersion on his hospitality. Indeed, Celia supposed that Lady Proctor had meant no such thing, since she had been giving every indication of enjoying herself very much.

The company was presently gathered in one of Julian's favourite rooms, a long gallery with mahogany panelling and a fireplace at either end. Before one of these their chairs were grouped in a semicircle around a table containing a late buffet supper. Lavinia, resplendent in a blue silk sari with the major part of her collection of semiprecious gems adorning her small hands, had chosen a lyre-backed satinwood chair at the centre of the little circle, where everyone else was obliged to face her. Nonetheless, neither she nor they seemed discomfited by her being the focus of attention. Indeed, it was a very comfortable gathering. No one, thought Celia, not even the Proctors, could fail to feel well looked after there.

She was somewhat relieved that the presence of the Proctors made it impossible for anyone to voice the obvious comparisons between them and the latest arrivals. The temptation to do so, and thereby establish an invisible but powerful barrier between family and visitors, would very likely pass before they had all gone to their beds that night. Still, Celia found a certain amusement of her own in the notion that the Proctors might appear quite conventional by comparison to the even more eccentric Danby-Davises.

She smiled faintly at the idea, and when she looked up a moment later she found Mr. Lambert watching her with much the same expression on his face. Upon that discovery, Celia cast her eyes downward again.

All the same, he moved his chair a little closer to hers to ask her if she had yet had the opportunity of conversing with the new arrivals.

"Only in the most fleeting way," she replied cautiously. "And you?"

"I had the honour of meeting them at breakfast this morning—when I was looking for *you*, incidentally. He was on the terrace when I arrived, in his shirtsleeves, breathing deeply and making odd jerking movements of his arms and legs. Henrietta—for so she insisted I address her—explained this to be an Oriental form of meditation. She said it aided the digestion."

Celia had to smile at the picture he conjured up and was almost sorry that she had gone out of her way—literally, taking the long path above Charmouth for her walk—to avoid meeting him at breakfast again.

"Did Mrs. Danby-Davis also perform these exercises?"

"No, one presumes her digestion is intact."

"Oh, dear. I wonder if we will find them next to invisible since they keep such early hours and do not join us at dinner. Or will they be underfoot in the most awkward way? In either case, they are an unsettling sort of houseguest, Kitty's notions of equality notwithstanding."

"Oh, I don't know," he replied, considering. "There are occasions when setting a cat or two among the pigeons can have useful consequences."

She frowned, unsure what he meant yet again. The only obvious interpretation was that the Danby-Davises made the Proctors look like models of decorum by comparison, but she could not consider it a good thing if this notion were carried so far that Phineas and Lavinia were turned into examples to be emulated. Apparently, Mr. Lambert had some deeper reason for favouring this result. When she tried to question him further, his attention was drawn away by Lady Proctor, who asked if it were true that he had a coffee plantation on the Amazon. He sent an apologetic look at Celia before correcting Lady Proctor's faulty geography.

"I have not gone so far as that, Lady Proctor," he assured her. "It is sugarcane that is raised at Indigo Hill, rather than coffee. Although coffee is grown in the hills." He smiled teasingly at her. "The mistake is a natural one, I daresay, considering that one uses the two products together."

"Do you not grow indigo, then?" Celia asked.

"Not so much as formerly. We produce enough to keep everyone on the place dressed in blue, but as a source of income sugar is—so to speak—sweeter."

Celia's schoolteacher mind was curious to learn more about a subject with which she was unfamiliar, but Sir Phineas diverted them all with a tale of a fire in a cane factory in India. Celia suspected the account was somewhat embroidered, though sufficiently engrossing to hold all their interests for half an hour.

Supper being concluded, the suggestion was made to retire to the library for the conclusion of the novel Kitty and Celia had begun reading aloud in turns. Reading had long been a favourite evening occupation among the Morlands, particularly given Kitty's interest in mediaeval tales, with which the anonymous author of *Waverley* so obligingly kept her supplied. They had, indeed, left off being enthralled by his *Ivanhoe* only when Mr. Lambert brought with him from London the latest sensational novel to shock the ton and Kitty had decreed that they might come back to the present long enough to read it. However, the prospect of reading anything at all seemed to Lady Proctor far too liable to achieve its intention of sending everyone off to a good night's rest. She countered with a proposal for a rubber of whist instead.

"But it's *Glenarvon*," Kitty told her, as if that explained all. "Nicky was very clever to be able to secure a copy. They are so much in demand."

Lady Proctor appeared unaware of the scandal Lady Caroline Lamb's roman à clef about her family and her relationship with Lord Byron had already achieved since its publication mere weeks before, or perhaps she knew about it after all and wished to avoid embarking on a discussion of social scandals. Either way, Lady Proctor stigmatised this style of entertainment in such a manner that Celia felt obliged to agree and profess herself perfectly content to concede the evening to those who preferred cards. Kitty was thus outnumbered and acquiesced, if a little petulantly, to the general preference.

"You should have stuck to your guns," Nicky Lambert whispered to Celia under cover of the move to the library. He was not, however, speaking out of consideration for Kitty's preferences. "She is a regular Captain Sharp and will doubtless take all of us mere flats for our remaining fortunes."

"Lady Proctor, do you mean? How do you know she is that?" Celia had to ask.

"Kitty and I were drafted into playing loo with the Proctors this afternoon. Even at a penny a point, she put us in Queer Street."

"Perhaps it is a skill they cultivated in order to support themselves in exile," Celia remarked, surprising a laugh out of Mr. Lambert.

Kitty, entering the library in front of them, turned and raised a quizzical eyebrow. She did not attempt to join them to discover what the joke was, however, and Celia could not help feeling a little relieved, if somewhat puzzled. She had made the remark unthinkingly, to be sure, her mind rather on the circumstances that might have led to that game of loo earlier. Had the Proctors found Kitty and Nicky together, or had Nicky and Kitty come upon them separately?

"Do stop fussing," Lady Proctor said just then to Julian, who was adjusting the leftover chairs into a neat pattern against the wall. "You will end up just like your father," she added cryptically, moving her own chair deliberately an inch farther from the table than it needed to be.

Julian smiled. "Do you mean, living to a ripe old age? I had no idea manhandling furniture contributed to his longevity."

"You know what I mean," Lavinia said, becoming a little peevish. "He always hated anything to be out of order and was forever doing servants' work. One could never find anything after he had finished straightening the writing desk or the bookshelves."

"I do beg your pardon," Julian said, abandoning his offensive activity to pull out a chair at the card table for Kitty. "I will endeavour to be less precise if that is what you prefer."

"Well, thank goodness for that," Mr. Lambert whispered again to Celia. When she looked puzzled, he explained, "If she's peevish, she can't concentrate so well as she might, and I may not be required to mortgage my plantation to her." When Celia sat down on the sofa next to the wall instead of taking a place at the table, he added, "Do you not play cards, Mrs. Morland?"

"Thank you, no."

"Pity."

He flashed one of his dazzling smiles before abandoning her to Sir Phineas, who also did not play. Kitty sat opposite Mr. Lambert, leaving Julian to partner Lady Proctor. Sir Phineas lowered himself carefully onto the sofa beside Celia and, when the sturdy old piece made no move to resist him, let out a sigh.

Celia smiled. "You do not care to take a hand, Sir Phineas?"

"Detest the silly game," he said, making a dismissive gesture with his handkerchief and sending a breath of his not unpleasant cologne towards Celia. "Whichever silly game it is. They're all the same."

"Your wife appears to enjoy cards, however."

"Oh, aye. Well, she's clever at that kind of thing." He seemed to take note of Celia for the first time and, winking impertinently at her, added, "Much prefer to sit with a pretty woman myself. Better still—a pretty, clever woman. Saves me from having to be clever, too, eh?"

Celia had to laugh at that. "Most gentlemen prefer not to be obliged to speak to a clever woman for fear of being made to appear dull-witted by comparison."

Sir Phineas waved his handkerchief again. "Pooh! Never pretended I was needle-witted myself. What would be the point of that? I'd only have to be proving my brilliance ever after."

"I do see that it would be easier if there were a length of

rough ground to cover, to be honest," Celia agreed, suppressing a smile at his expense.

"That's the ticket," Sir Phineas agreed, shifting himself slightly on the sofa to face Celia without the barrier of his shirt points coming between them. He was as splendidly arrayed as ever this evening in a pale blue coat, dark grey pantaloons, and a pink watered-silk waistcoat with pearl buttons to set it all off. "It don't pay to bamboozle people. It catches you up in the end. Besides, I never could keep a secret."

"But I thought—" Celia could not go on to pry into Sir Phineas's past and stumbled out an apology. "I do beg your pardon."

"Quite all right, m'dear. I know what you were going to say. How did I manage to elope with Lavinia all those years ago if I couldn't keep our plans to myself? Well, I will tell you."

Celia knew she ought not to listen. However, Sir Phineas's ability to tell a story had been amply proven, and she could not resist.

"How could I keep the secret, you wonder?" Sir Phineas asked rhetorically, gazing off into some private source of inspiration. "Well, I didn't. That's the answer! If I had been clever, or a gentleman, I would never have told Lavinia how I felt about her, and she would never have told me, and we would never have eloped. She might be Julian's mother today, and I would be only a retired East India Company clerk."

"Then it is just as well you cannot keep a secret," Celia said, amused.

"That's the truth of it." He frowned as a cloud crossed the clear skies of reminiscence. "James could, of course, keep a secret. Close, James was. Close-mouthed, clutch-fisted, and cold as a herring. Weren't acquainted with James, were you?" he asked abruptly, looking to see if she were offended by his unvarnished opinion.

Celia shook her head to answer both questions.

"So you see," he rumbled on, "why your humble servant

might have looked to Lavinia like the answer to a maiden's—well, a matron's—prayer. Of course, I was a good-looking buck in those days. Not so handsome as Julian or Lambert there, but more than one pretty girl looked twice when I walked by."

Celia followed his glance at the card table, where the first rubber had just run its course and Lady Proctor was remarking to Julian that she admired a man who played a cautious game but he need not be quite so slow to make his moves. Nicky forestalled an apology from Julian by assuring Lady Proctor that it was only her extraordinary skill that made the rest of them look like slow-tops. She gave him an assessing glance, but he kept his countenance. In another moment she was giggling girlishly and making him change chairs with Julian so that they could be partners.

"I'm certain the ladies still admire you," Celia replied tactfully to Sir Phineas's remark, which made him give a snort of laughter.

"Right you are again, m'dear. But not for the same reason nowadays, eh? You look at Lambert quick enough, with his rogue's eye and quick tongue, but you'd only laugh at an old peacock like me."

Celia wished he would not insist on setting Nicky Lambert up as an example, particularly when she was all too aware of that gentleman's charms. There was an edge to her voice when she responded, "I hope I would not be so rude, Sir Phineas."

He cast her an appraising glance over his billowing cravat. "No, I daresay you would do no more than smile in such a way as to make me believe you admired me, even if you thought something quite different. At this very moment, I venture you are wishing I would not keep pointing out the obvious to you, but you do not say so aloud." He chuckled and patted Celia's arm. "You should have been a diplomat, m'dear—eh?"

"I regret I would not be allowed to serve, sir," Celia replied to divert his thoughts. "I should have to be a diplomat's wife."

"That's the truth. Lavinia would have made a fine diplomat's wife." He gave Celia a shrewd glance from his pale blue eyes that held more intelligence, she was beginning to see, than he admitted to. "You don't think so, do you? But she would have, years ago. I wasn't clever enough to rise to that caste, however, so she had to be content with getting rich instead. I didn't have to be clever to do that. You see, getting rich in India in those days was as easy as breathing. You got up in the morning, opened the windows, and the rupees came flying in."

Celia laughed. "I am persuaded there was more to it than that, sir."

"Oh, well . . . " He shrugged as much as his tightly fitted coat would allow. "It's true that I had to grease a few palms, butter up a few suppliers, sweet-talk the ladies with titles in front of their names into patronising my little establishment. But it didn't take the baby long to grow too big for its nursery and to acquire some siblings. No, no—not long at all for a small drygoods shop to turn into a chain of warehouses supplying a select purveyor in each of the big cities—nor to bamboozle a great many ladies with titles into thinking they had discovered the perfect shop for English goods in India and bragging about it to their friends."

"That must have kept you very busy, sir."

"Not at all. I was clever enough to learn one lesson at a time. One of the first I learned, even before Lavinia and I were married—" He glanced at her to see if she were shocked and, apparently satisfied that she was not, went on. "The first lesson, I say, was that it don't do to let a wife get bored or lonely."

He gave her another appraising glance and asked, "You are not married, girl?"

"I am a widow, sir."

"Ah," he said. "That'll explain it."

Celia was not certain precisely what that explained but did not have the opportunity to ask before he said, "Your husband was related to the little Kitty? You've the same name, haven't you?"

"Yes, Harry was her brother."

"Harry, eh? Good English name, that. I've never met a Harry I didn't take to right off."

Celia smiled. "Neither have I."

He laughed at that and asked her a few more questions that were personal but not prying, and Celia found herself talking more than she usually did about herself. She even dug Harry's watch out of her pocket and showed it to the old knight, who examined it carefully.

"A sailor's watch. Nice piece, too. Daresay it keeps good time even when it gets seawater in it."

"Yes," Celia said.

She did not explain that it had indeed been exposed to the sea, but, unlike Harry, it had survived. Nonetheless, Sir Phineas seemed to understand that he had touched on a sensitive memory and patted her arm again before tactfully changing the subject.

"I took on people I could trust," he said, returning to the tale of how he had made his fortune, "and let them do the work, while Lavinia and I gadded about—always together, mind you—looking at palaces and acting like nabobs. Nobody knew the difference back then between the real nobs and those of us in trade. We were all foreigners, after all, and so naturally superior—we liked to think—to everyone else."

Celia had to admire Sir Phineas's calm acceptance of things that anyone else might have wasted time in deploring. She considered it very likely that he had done more to lessen friction between the English and the Indians than any hundred missionaries and made a good life for himself and his wife at the same time. Indeed, she thought it also likely that it was Lavinia who had been foremost in his consideration all along. He must have cushioned every tiny blow for her then, just as he was careful now to find her the most comfortable chair and to keep her supplied with plenty of whist partners even when he himself had no interest in the silly game.

"You must have been very happy in India," she said to him, her mind among imagined hill stations with pleasant breezes playing among the bougainvillaea and mysteriously spicy smells drifting up from the kitchen where an army of servants kept one in luxurious comfort. "Is that why you stayed so long?"

"No, m'dear," said Sir Phineas, bringing her back to earth, "we stayed because no one here would give us the time of day."

"Oh, dear!" said Celia, apostrophising herself once again for being a fool and forgetting the obvious. "I do beg your pardon again." But he seemed not to take it amiss.

"Quite all right, m'dear. It's a treat to come across anyone—especially a female—who has so little care for the old scandal, and who don't put on missish airs when it's mentioned. People here mostly have longer memories."

Another picture came to Celia's mind, of Sir Phineas imposing his bulk between tiny Lavinia and a gabble of gossip-mongers so that she would not hear and be hurt by what was said about her.

"Has that been difficult for you?"

"No, no. Not for myself. Don't care what they say, for myself. It bothered Lavinia at first, though, which is why we decided to come here. Thought to exorcise the old ghosts once and for all."

"I trust you may do so."

Jeffreys entered with the tea tray, putting a halt to the whist game, which had been getting a little heated. In the relative silence that followed, Celia did not expect him to reply. But as Sir Phineas rose ponderously, leaning on her arm, he smiled and patted her sleeve once again.

"With your help, m'dear, I daresay we will," he said. "I daresay."

7

CAREFUL QUESTIONING OF the servants the next morning informed Julian that he would be most likely to find the Proctors alone in the middle of the afternoon. Weather permitting, they took tea on the terrace, a habit they had acquired in India but which no one else in the house shared. Julian shook his head, allowing himself to deplore privately the peculiarities of his guests, which he was perfectly willing to make allowances for. Nonetheless, this resulted in a very strange sort of house party, with people amusing themselves individually instead of in company. He was beginning to appreciate the virtues of a woman like Celia Morland. Although she might not take part in whatever activity was planned, at least she kept those that did company and never made her philosophy or religion or whatever it might be called the excuse for absenting herself.

He had found her dull in the past, Julian had to confess; but of late Celia had begun to seem subtle, rather a gentlewoman, in fact, who might be quiet but was always considerate of others and displayed her generous nature in unobtrusive ways. Indeed, it was difficult not to make use of her to accomplish those little duties everyone else found uninteresting or intrusive. Not that she was interfering—indeed, she never volunteered her time or services or made any show of helping out. Julian hoped she had not been made to feel as if she had to earn her keep. She was as much an honoured guest as anyone else and certainly more pleasant to have around than most.

Now that he thought further on it, she was a quietly beautiful woman, as well. It was odd that he had never noticed that before. Perhaps she had changed somehow, of late. He would have to observe her more carefully.

At the moment, however, Julian had other things on his mind, and they were taking on some urgency. He hurried down the hall, relieved to see the Danby-Davises nowhere about, and decided to take a shortcut through the west wing and out the servants' staircase, which gave onto the walk beside the terrace. On his way, however, he decided to traverse the picture gallery, since no one else was in the habit of going there. He certainly did not count on finding his betrothed.

Kitty was standing in the light cast by the sun coming through the leaded panes of the windows on one side of the gallery. She gazed at a painting with a rapt expression on her face and looked much like a picture herself in a pale yellow gown with a great deal of lace at the bodice and hem. She must have picked up that contemplative posture from her sister-in-law, thought Julian, for Kitty rarely stood still more than a few seconds at a time when unaware of being observed. Either that, or the picture she was looking at held some unusual fascination for her. Julian came up quietly behind and looked to see what it might be.

It was a portrait of Lavinia, painted just before her marriage and showing her in a dress remarkably like Kitty's except for the old-fashioned cut. Lavinia wore a singular lack of jewelled ornament other than her betrothal ring, ostentatiously displayed, and a setter puppy with a jewelled collar gazed blissfully up at her from a cushion beside her chair. A few days ago, Julian would have been hard put to see the resemblance between the present Lady Proctor and the young Miss Lavinia Stanford. Now he realised that the smile—coquettish but remarkably sweet—had not changed at all. The puppy's expression was somewhat reminiscent of Sir Phineas. Julian dismissed this unworthy thought.

In any case, despite his impatience to be about his business, Julian found the back of Kitty's neck far more interesting than Lavinia's vanished youth. He bent over slightly, just enough to touch his nose to her hair and capture the delicate odour of soap which he preferred to any exotic perfume. He moved his head a little, touching his cheek to the soft, pale gold curls, then turned to kiss her neck.

Kitty jumped. "Oh, good gracious—Julian! How you startled me."

A little irritated that she had not even been aware of his presence, he stepped back. "I beg your pardon, I'm sure."

Kitty was instantly contrite and threw her arms around his neck. "Oh, no, Julian, dear. It is I who beg *your* pardon. I must have fallen into one of my silly moods. I daresay I would not have heard the crack of doom."

Julian smiled and disentangled himself. "I trust I am not that. Were you admiring Lady Proctor's portrait?"

Kitty turned back to the painting. "Well, of course she was not Lady Proctor then. She was pretty, though, wasn't she? Do you think she might have stayed that way had she been—that is, had she remained happily married and not run off with Sir Phineas?"

"She certainly would not have stayed seventeen for very long. She cannot be said to have aged gracefully, I suppose, but I see no reason that she would otherwise have turned out any differently. Besides, I do not find her all that repellent after all, do you?"

Kitty looked at him curiously. "Well, I suppose she is pleasant enough. Do you *like* her, Julian?"

He shrugged. "I do not dislike her."

"But she—I mean, she did your father a great wrong."

Reminded of his business, Julian frowned and was about to make his excuses and be on his way when Kitty said, "Oh, do forgive me again, Julian! I did not mean to bring up a painful subject, but . . . from my point of view, of course, it was a good thing that Lavinia did leave your father, for otherwise he would not have married your mother, and I would not have you."

The elegance of this logic was lost on Julian, but he suffered Kitty to kiss him and smile tremulously until he forgave her for her entirely imaginary fault. Then he tore himself away—not so soon as he would have liked—and turned towards the door, trying not to look as if he were fleeing from her.

"Julian, mayn't I go with you?" Kitty cried, hurrying after him down the gallery.

"Only as far as the landing, my dear. There is some business I must attend to, and I am later about it than I intended. Kitty, please do *not* apologise again. You did not detain me, except in the most pleasant way . . . Oh, the devil take it. I will see you at dinner, Kitty."

He kissed her quickly and hurried away, leaving Kitty looking forlorn on the landing. It was as much as he could do not to return. He would have liked nothing more than to listen to more of her absurd apologies and soothe her with caresses and kind words—but not now.

"China tea!" Sir Phineas announced in that way he had of heralding the subject of conversation while making no subsequent contribution to it.

Julian was relieved to find the Proctors apparently settled for the rest of the afternoon on the terrace overlooking the garden. When Sir Phineas made no further comment, Lavinia was obliged to explain that Jeffreys had been so bold as to offer them green tea instead of black, a thing Phineas was not at all accustomed to.

"I'm certain we have black tea on hand, sir. I daresay Jeffreys thought you might like—er, a choice."

"Oh, he did," Lavinia assured him. "I mean—he did have the black tea and brought it at once. It's just that we are accustomed to it, you know, living in India . . . and one gets into one's little habits."

"Of course," Julian agreed, to put Lavinia out of her uncertainty about whether she might have offended either her host or, worse yet, her host's butler. "Do you take it with milk or lemon?"

"Oh, milk, certainly," Lavinia said, her husband being content with levelling an offended look at Julian for even suggesting there might be an alternative.

"Guernsey or Jersey?" Julian continued.

Lavinia looked puzzled, so he explained, "We have several breeds of cattle on the estate, most of which give excellent milk."

At that, Sir Phineas let out a guffaw and leaned over creakingly to slap Julian on the knee.

"Very good, my boy! Capital joke."

Lavinia giggled, pleased to have a congenial atmosphere restored, and offered Julian a cup of tea (Indian) with milk (breed indeterminate). Julian maintained his patience as best he could until at last, their being down to the last cream-cake, he was able to introduce the subject he had come expressly to raise.

"I wonder, Lady Proctor, if I may speak to you in my study for a few moments. Privately."

Sir Phineas sent him a sharp look at that, but Lavinia intercepted it. Julian was interested to observe that they seemed to communicate a whole conversation between themselves without saying a word. A moment later, Sir Phineas shrugged, and Lavinia told Julian she would be happy to go with him now if he wished. Julian bowed, casting a last thoughtful look at Sir Phineas, who had picked up the newspaper with an air of unconcern, and opened the door for Lavinia to precede him out of the room.

Despite having planned carefully what he wanted to say, Julian found himself stiffening up before he began. He offered Lavinia the most comfortable chair in the library, but she declined in favour of the sofa which, he realised too late, she preferred because it allowed her feet to touch the floor. He offered her a cushion, then realised that any further efforts to put her at ease might be construed as fussiness. He also knew better than to introduce any small talk, at which he was singularly inept. Instead, he picked up the book he had left out on the desk. He hesitated for a moment, looking at the book as if he had never seen it before. Then he handed it to her. She glanced at it curiously, then at Julian, without taking the book from him.

"Forgive me, Lady Proctor, if what I am about to say raises uncomfortable memories."

"Do call me Lavinia, my dear boy," she said, reaching out her hand to lay it over his. "I have nothing to hide, I assure you, despite what you may have heard. Do let us be honest with each other and take no offence at hurts that are long past."

She smiled up at him, the slight lopsidedness of her mouth emphasised by the paint hastily applied to it. He offered her the book again, this time folding her outstretched hand over it.

"Lavinia, this is my father's dairy. Have you ever seen it before?"

She turned the book over gingerly, as if it were an artifact from an Egyptian tomb. "Oh, not for many years. I knew James kept one. He never offered to let me read it, though."

"Would you be good enough to turn to the page marked with a ribbon and read it now."

Lavinia did as she was told, and for a moment afterwards there was silence in the room. Then she closed the book abruptly and looked up, still dry-eyed, at Julian.

"So you have known all along."

"No, I only recently discovered the diary. My father had hidden it away with some old estate bills, which I disturbed only accidentally while attempting to make that drawer in the desk move more smoothly."

Lavinia smiled faintly, and Julian guessed that she was thinking again of those habits of his which she found overly fastidious rather than merely orderly, as he himself had always considered them. Well, he could not help what people thought.

"What happened to the child?" he asked, more abruptly than he had intended.

Her face fell pathetically, as if mere paint could not hold it together against strong emotion.

"He died."

Tears filled her eyes, but she made no move to wipe them away. Julian immediately regretted his tone and took out a handkerchief, handing it to her.

"Forgive me."

She looked up, clutching the handkerchief. "I never knew him—never even saw him—but he was my only child. Phineas and I were never able to have one."

Julian said nothing, and after a moment she went on.

"James was terribly upset. He so much wanted an heir, and when the doctor told him I might not have another, he was . . . he was angry with me. I was only nineteen then, and he must have been thinking ahead to all the years he would have to be married to me with no possibility of the heir he wanted more than a wife."

Julian frowned, annoyed at himself for never having considered this point of view before.

"I'm so sorry, Julian. I do not mean to make your father out to be a monster. He was . . . he was very good to me, even after that. Or at least he tried to be. I'm afraid I did not try quite so hard. James was good to me, giving me everything I needed, except—well—he was not affectionate. Do you understand? I did so need affection. Then Phineas came along and he was so different . . . I could not help falling in love with him." At last, the tears began to flow silently, making tiny tracks through the rouge on her cheeks. "Phineas gave me that affection, you see."

At a loss what to do, Julian stepped back as if to give Lavinia a little privacy, then perceived that this was precisely what his father would have done instead of offering his wife that simple affection she craved. Julian moved forward once more to sit beside Lavinia on the sofa and put his arm around her. He felt deucedly awkward, but it was the least he could do. Lavinia seemed to be grateful for the gesture.

There was a loud knock on the door. Lavinia jumped up and collided with Julian, who kept his arm around her anyway as Sir Phineas opened the door and marched into the study, coming to a lowering halt in front of the sofa.

"What's going on here, eh?" he demanded of Julian, at the same time scowling at his wife. "What's the matter, pet, eh? Eh?"

Lavinia stuffed Julian's handkerchief into her bosom and reached out a hand to pat her husband's sleeve.

"Now, don't overset yourself, Phineas. I'm quite all right."

"No, you ain't," Sir Phineas announced, drawing himself up to his full height and saying, with some dignity, to Julian, "You have upset my wife, sir. Be so good as to go away and trouble her no more."

Julian found himself unable to meet Sir Phineas's stern gaze entirely without guilt and said nothing, but bowed and left the room. Closing the door behind him, he caught a glimpse of the two old lovers together on the sofa, Sir Phineas muttering something to his wife and wiping her cheeks gently with his own handkerchief as she smiled tenderly up at him.

Half an hour later Julian was riding away from the manor, where his groom was in a state of shock after being spoken to so brusquely by his heretofore considerate employer. Mrs. Milsom had happened to be in the kitchen garden at the time and also wondered what the master was about, to go off like that by himself in such a hurry.

Julian was not himself precisely sure where he was going or why, but he felt a need to get away from home and to exhaust himself in some kind of physical exercise. The beauties of the early spring landscape were lost on him. Although he was half-conscious that the ground was hard from last night's rain, he was blind to the new leaves on the hedgerows and the primroses along the lane. By the time he had reached the Boar's Head in Axminster, he was physically exhausted, as he'd hoped to be, but his mind was racing.

The child died, he told himself. *Leave it alone.*

But Julian was incapable of letting a thing alone once he had determined to do something about it, and he refused to depend on someone else's assurances that it would be taken care of. If he was in the habit of letting others manage his affairs, he would still be finding the home-farm accounts short every month because his bailiff was cheating him, and he would still be having to replace the wall on the west border of the estate every week because he had not waited there one night to discover that the farmer on the other side was helping himself to stones to line his well.

"How may I serve you, sir?" a voice broke in.

Julian refocused his eyes to find the landlord of the Boar's Head standing beside him and realised that he must have seated himself in the taproom without being aware of his actions.

"Ale, sir?" the landlord asked, stifling whatever opinion he may have had of his guest's abstraction. "You look as if you've had a long ride, and there's nothing like ale to take the edge off a thirst, is there, sir?"

"Yes, ale. Thank you."

The landlord bowed and went off, reappearing a moment later with a tankard, from which Julian took a long swallow before letting his mind escape again.

He should have asked Lavinia if the child had been baptised. If it had a name, it might be easier to trace. More than likely, of course, it would have been called James, or Edward, his father's second name. Or even Julian, if that was the name James had been reserving for his heir. James had thought in those terms, as Lavinia had suggested.

She had been right about other things as well. For the first time in years, Julian let memories of his childhood come to the surface of his consciousness, memories he had buried deep inside him because they were invariably of the same kind of scene. There was his first attempt to ride a pony, for example. Julian had thought he was doing well, and old Sam had encouraged him to "hang on, young sir!" Julian's father, however, had watched him with a scowl and corrected every fault in terms that made Julian feel he was the most awkward child that had ever been born. Then, when he fell and could not help but cry from the sharp pain of a stone on his knee, his father had given Julian a disgusted look, leaving him there on the ground to be picked up and carried inside by Sam, who assured him he had done very well for a first go.

Sam's words, however kindly meant, were lies, or so Julian was certain. Only his father told the truth. Julian was fourteen before it occurred to him that there might after all be some grace in his father's graceless son. Julian had gone to spend the week with a school friend, whose father was everything James was not. He'd congratulated Julian on a school prize he had won in mathematics.

"Beat every other boy all hollow, I hear," said Mr. Gilmore, and Julian had wondered how he knew that.

It was only later that his friend, Henry Gilmore, told him that James had added the news about the prize to the letter he sent with Julian to the Gilmores. But when Julian had told his father earlier about the prize, James said he had not heard about it and, anyway, it only showed Julian would have to work harder to win the next one. He couldn't just expect these things to fall in his lap, could he? He had to earn them.

Julian took another draught of the ale, hoping to swallow these unpleasant memories along with it. Perhaps if he drank enough, it would help. He wondered if Lavinia had been able to drown *her* memories, until he reminded her so unthinkingly of her own unhappiness with James. Of course, she had Phineas to help her forget . . . and Julian had Kitty . . . Why, then, could he not forget, too?

He gazed out the taproom window for a moment into the churchyard next door, where the sexton was weeding some of the graves. Julian watched him thoughtfully for a few minutes, then got up, tossed a coin on the table, and went out the back door. He hadn't investigated this particular churchyard yet. It wouldn't hurt to ask.

8

CELIA WAS UNACCOUNTABLY disappointed to find that Mr. Lambert did not after all contrive to meet her on her early walks. Consequently, one particularly warm morning several days later she decided to take a horse out of the stables rather than exert herself on foot. Feeling more than usually restive, she did not take her regular route, which was sheltered from the sea by the line of trees at the edge of the Hardwicke property. Instead, she rode the mare over the Spittles towards the cliffs to the east of Lyme Regis, where the breeze was brisker and the path closer to the edge. As the smell of the sea grew strong in her nostrils, she found herself urging the mare more quickly towards it.

Why should he come out to meet you, after all, the sensible part of her insisted, *when Kitty is always there, pretty as an illustration from one of her favourite novels and more than happy to flirt with him—or to share secrets with him?*

Furthermore, her sensible self informed her, what had really disappointed her was seeing Kitty and Nicky alone together the morning before, earlier than either of them was accustomed to be awake and abroad. It was not that Celia had wanted to find them so. In fact, she had begun to think the idea of their running away together had after all been a foolish notion, the figment of her own romantic imagination.

Nevertheless, there was no denying she had seen them. She had walked out the sun-parlour door into the garden, thinking to take the path that ran from the gate in the hedge to the cliffs. There, on the bench shielded from the house by the brick wall, sat Nicky with his arm unmistakably around Kitty's shoulder. Kitty had apparently been crying, because she had her handkerchief in her hand, but Celia did not wait to be sure. She turned swiftly, hoping she had not been heard, and went back through the house to take her walk in another direction.

When she returned neither Kitty nor Nicky were anywhere to be seen, and Celia experienced a momentary dread that they really had eloped. Then Kitty had come down to lunch and picked at her food, saying nothing to anyone. She had not then seemed much like one of her princess heroines, palely loitering, in wait for her knight to spirit her away on a white steed. Celia tried to imagine herself in the same situation and was forced to admit that she would probably behave in the same listless, preoccupied manner.

When Nicky did not appear for dinner, either, Celia breathed a sigh of relief that he was not off somewhere making arrangements for an abduction. Kitty remarked petulantly over her sweet that he had gone off to see his father without so much as taking his leave of her.

"I should not think he needed to apologise for visiting his father," Celia had remarked, unsure whether to be pleased or annoyed that Mr. Lambert had not confided his intentions to her either. Why should he be considerate of her forebodings, when he had no idea she had them? She learned only later from Mrs. Milsom that Mr. Lambert had received a summons from home that his father, who had been ill for some time, had taken a turn for the worse.

"Only doing his duty as a son," the housekeeper had remarked as she and Celia sat comfortably in the kitchen planning menus for the following week—yet another chore that Kitty preferred to leave to those more qualified than herself. "I doubt there's any love between them any more. The old man gave all his attention to the older boys all Mr. Nicholas's life. Kept telling him he'd amount to nothing, so why should he bother to educate him or set him up in business or buy him a commission."

"Had he no interest he particularly wished to pursue?" Celia asked.

"Oh my, yes. He took an interest in any number of things. As a boy, Mr. Nicholas was always hanging about the stables, even the kitchens, asking how this or that was done and wanting to give it a go himself. Don't know if any of those things took, but he was certainly quick to learn. I daresay they've come in handy since he's had his own land and tenants to concern himself with, even if it is in the Indies. They must need horseshoes there, too."

Celia had no idea if any of this was true, and although she was quite certain she ought not to listen to below-stairs gossip, she nodded encouragingly just the same.

"My sister was in service at Woodbridge for more than twenty years," Mrs. Milsom explained, relieving Celia of her first qualm at least.

The housekeeper was a stern-looking woman in her fifties who nonetheless took enough pleasure in life to look at it out of a pair of lively, curious brown eyes. She crossed out fricassee of chicken on Tuesday's dinner menu and substituted fricandeau of veal before laying that sheet of paper facedown on top of Monday's and going on with her tale.

"Sadie always said Mr. Nicholas only stayed on at home for his mother's sake, for he was her youngest and her favourite. But even that couldn't keep him there after he and his dad had one almighty row a few years back. Sadie had the night off—which she's never stopped being sorry about—and so didn't hear the details, but she thought the old man had started in on Mrs. Lambert for spoiling the boy and making what he called a useless fop out of him.

"Well, the lad was man enough not to take that, and the very same night—after midnight, it was, Sadie remembers, because she was just coming in—he took off down the road with nothing but the clothes on his back and the horse he was riding. He sent the horse back, too.

"Shall we have peas or beans Wednesday? There's some lovely peas in the garden that should be ready to pick by then."

"I'm sorry. What did you say?"

Celia's mind, caught up in the picture of Nicky Lambert setting out to make his fortune—a task he had apparently accomplished with ease—quite failed to comprehend the introduction of peas and beans into the conversation. Anna Milsom gave her a shrewd look. "Peas it is, then. May as well take advantage of what's offered when it's fresh."

The mare had become skittish because they were so near the edge of the cliff, so Celia dismounted and tied the horse to a tree. She sat down on the rocky ledge and looked down towards the strand. The tide was out and the sandy expanse at its broadest and most inviting. Celia tied her cloak to her saddle and began scrambling down the path along the side of the cliff. It was an inelegant descent, harking back to the days when Kitty had been able to persuade Celia to postpone chores in favour of a basket luncheon on the beach. Celia glanced around to see if she had been observed. Some distance away on the sand she could see the figure of a man, but he had his back to her. He had abandoned his boots and stockings and was walking barefoot along the water's edge, his breeches rolled up almost to his knees. Something about him struck Celia as familiar, and when he bent to pick something up from the sand, she knew who it was from the grace of the movement and his attitude as he stood perfectly still turning the object over in his hand. When she turned to retreat the way she had come, he saw her and waved, then started down the beach towards her. Not knowing what else to do, she was forced to wait until he caught up.

"Good morning, Mrs. Morland. What a delight to meet you here. This beach is not, I think, on your usual morning itinerary."

Celia could not help looking down at Mr. Lambert's bare toes, which he seemed to have no modesty about. They were as brown as his slender hands, indicating that he frequently went about unshod. She had a sudden, rather pleasant picture of him walking along a palm-fringed beach in Jamaica. It had to be an inaccurate picture, of course. He must work more than he played at home.

"It seems to be on your route, however," she replied, raising her eyes just to his collar. She would do better, she thought, if she did not look into his eyes and if she did not think about Kitty, but simply approached this as an unexpectedly pleasant encounter with a friend.

"Yes," he said. "I discovered the path down the cliff several days ago—or I should say rediscovered it, for I used it often when I was a boy but did not know if it was still here. I was obliged to ride over to Woodbridge for a few days, however, and could not return to explore until this morning. A delicious morning, is it not?—as one imagines the first dawn on earth might have been. Think of God's surprise when he saw it."

"I trust you found your father improved?" Celia asked, falling into step when he turned and began walking back up the beach the way he had come. He frowned and did not answer for a moment, making her sorry that she had destroyed his blithe mood. In her eagerness to learn more about his family and therefore about him, she had once again spoken without ample consideration.

"He is as well as can be expected. He is dying."

"Oh, I'm so sorry," Celia said softly.

Any last thought of prying into his business with Kitty evaporated as sympathy enveloped Celia. Anna Milsom had said his father was unwell. Indeed, she had implied that it was the reason for Mr. Lambert's recent return to England, but Celia had not thought to enquire into the nature of the old man's malady. Surely someone else at the manor would have known? She ought to have asked, Celia told herself, casting about for something to say to atone for her apparent insensitivity. Then Mr. Lambert smiled at her.

"Why should you be sorry? There is nothing you can do about it. Nor I, for that matter."

"I only meant—that is, I'm sorry that . . . " She wanted to say, *I'm sorry that you have been made unhappy*, but that seemed not only presumptuous, but selfish. "... I am sorry to hear it."

"He is over eighty and has been ill for many years," Mr. Lambert replied, his voice steady but the lilt gone out of it. "He recognises no one, not even my mother. Is it heartless of me to say I wish for nothing but a speedy release for him? Or selfish to say that I hope I will be able to remember him as he was when I was a boy rather than as the frail, helpless creature he is now?"

"Not at all. Harry's—my father-in-law also died at an advanced age, and my husband had a great dread of suffering in the same way. I think that must be why he was so heedless physically. He was almost daring fate to do the same thing to him."

He stopped in his tracks for a moment to look at her, and she suddenly realised what she had said. How had she come to say anything so private to him? She had not even known she thought it. She could only suppose that crises in one's life tended to draw one's friends nearer. She met his look. She could not deny what she had said, but he seemed to understand.

"Kitty tells me you lost your parents at a very early age," he said gently.

"Yes," she said, moving on so that he would follow. "I don't remember them at all. I suppose it's best that way."

"I think it must often be so. Do you know anything about them?"

"Not much more than their names and ages. I have some books of my father's and my mother's wedding ring. There were also a half-dozen letters. They weren't separated for more than a few days in the whole time of their marriage, which was brief in any case, so the letters don't say very much. Still, I can picture—or I imagine I can—from the ordinary things they wrote about in the letters, what their life together was like."

He smiled. "Have you ever told Kitty about this?"

"I don't think I have," she said, surprised again at the

trusting way she revealed to him what she would never have thought of telling Kitty. Celia supposed it was because she always thought before telling Kitty anything, and Nicky seemed to draw out secrets as easily as if they had not been firmly fastened inside her for years.

"Why do you say that?" Celia asked.

"Because according to her, you have no imagination."

"Well, of all the unjust things to say!" Celia protested, laughing just the same, because she had no doubt that Kitty had said just that.

"So I told her," he said, "particularly since she had just told me that you are an author. Perhaps she imagines that you write mailcoach timetables. Not that those aren't sometimes highly imaginative. The stage I took down from London promised to reach Exeter by ten o'clock, but it was nearly noon by the time we arrived. Yet, the driver did not look in the least contrite."

Celia smiled, not so much at the jest but in gratitude for his giving her a moment thereby to prepare herself for whatever he was going to say about her poetry, which she now had no doubt he had read. It struck her, too, that she no longer found everything he said so baffling. Perhaps they were coming to an understanding after all. Perhaps she could even, sometime soon, broach the subject of his feelings for Kitty and surprise the truth out of him.

"I read some of your poems," he said, no longer unexpectedly. When Celia did not reply, he looked down at the sand as if, oddly enough, he were the one who was sensitive about her writing. "I particularly liked the one about the window," he said, and glanced up, quizzing her. "One so easily overlooks the obvious, everyday things one sees from one's window that their beauty is lost. You recaptured that beauty."

"Thank you."

"Were you speaking of your window at the cottage?"

"Yes."

Celia felt herself blush at that. Somehow the identification of the real window seemed a more intimate admission than anything she might say about the meaning of the poem.

"I should add," he went on in a bantering tone, "that when I asked Kitty if she had read it, she said that she had never seen anything so marvelous from that window."

Celia had to laugh. "And she accuses me of a lack of imagination?"

"Oh, she didn't mean to be unkind. Indeed, she looks up to you for your intelligence and common sense."

"My dullness and predictability, you mean."

"Yes, I assured her she was all out there."

His grin told Celia she had made her own trap and fallen into it. She had to force herself not to laugh again as she put her hands on her hips and castigated him. "You needn't be so agreeable."

"What would you have me do?" he asked in mock offence. "Disagree with her on no evidence but my own instincts? Or fly to your defence and risk a jealous tantrum?"

Oh, dear—how could she have forgotten? Celia's newly merry mood dissolved with the remembrance of reality. What was it about him that made one think one the centre of his world?

He seemed to sense her change of mood and stopped to face her, frowning.

"Celia—"

She took an involuntary step backwards. He reached out to catch her arm, and she realised that she had stepped into a pool of seawater. He let her go as soon as she regained her balance, and she was grateful to see that he was not going to pursue whatever he had intended to say in that disquieting tone of voice.

"Look here," he remarked instead. "You seem to have disturbed the anemones."

He bent down and gently stroked the green strands of what looked to be seaweed clinging to the rocky edge of the pool. The strands clung to his finger greedily. Celia laughed.

"You are well and thoroughly captured."

"It will let go when it finds it can't eat me."

He wiggled his finger and the green tentacles contracted again into the body of the anemone. "I'm always surprised at the life along these shores."

Mr. Lambert stood up and brushed his hands against his breeches with a fine disregard for the sensibilities of his valet who, Celia had also learned from Anna Milsom, was named Thomas and had crossed the sea several times in his employer's service. Celia supposed he was accustomed to Nicky's careless habits.

"After living in Jamaica," Mr. Lambert went on, "I find it wonderful that any sort of creature can survive, much less thrive, in these cold waters."

"They survive because they must," Celia said. "They have not the choice of removing to the tropics."

"Why do *you* stay?"

"I?" She was a little taken aback. "Why, because this is my home." She laughed. "How ingenuous that sounds—particularly since I was not born here and no one who was, except the Morlands, will ever accept that it is my home. But I must confess I have never considered living anywhere else since I came here."

"Not even after your husband died? Did you feel no need to begin again, to put the past behind you?"

"The past is not always something that must be got over. Sometimes it is pleasant to remember, and to be reminded by what is around one—what is just outside one's window, in fact."

"I see."

He sounded oddly regretful. Celia longed to know whether this was because he regretted that he himself had not been closer to his family, but she did not know how to ask. She said nothing, and they walked along the edge of the water for a while in silence. The beach began to be less sandy and more rock-strewn, with tiny tidal pools amongst the rocks that held still other, livelier sea-dwelling creatures. He turned over a snail shell that was revealed to house a large crab, and Celia wet her own feet chasing after it when it fell out. She laughed when it scuttled along the sand into another pool to escape her.

"You must take your boots and stockings off now as well," he told her, but she shook her head.

"Certainly not! You live in uncivilised parts and may be excused for eccentric behaviour on those grounds. I must live here and risk encountering some neighbour who would not hesitate to spread the word of my indiscretion. Besides, these boots are used to far worse treatment."

"I cannot imagine your ever being indiscreet."

"Oh, dear. You do not make discretion sound like a virtue."

"Of course it is. Otherwise, indiscretion would not be so attractive. Don't you find it so?"

"I rarely find it at all."

"I don't believe that. Have you never taken your shoes off out-of-doors?"

"Yes, of course, when I was a child, but that was different . . . "

"And did Harry Morland never tempt you into indiscretions—or commit any number himself for love of Celia? Knowing Kitty, I cannot believe that a brother of hers would not exercise considerable imagination to win the woman he had set his heart on."

Celia felt herself blushing again, not for Harry's indiscretions, but at the realisation that she was flirting—she, Celia Morland, actually flirting!—with Nicholas Lambert. She must have been doing it all along. No wonder Kitty made a habit of it. This behaviour was far easier to fall into than to resist, particularly when he sounded as if he meant every nonsensical thing he said.

"Speaking of eccentric behaviour—" he began.

"Were we?"

"You brought up the subject, may I remind you. But it occurred to me this morning whom Henrietta Danby-Davis reminds me of."

"Whom?" Celia asked, fascinated that there could be another such creature in the world.

"Lady Hester Stanhope. Did you ever meet her?"

"No, although I know of her. When I was in Wales I met some relations of Miss Williams, the companion Lady Hester took with her to the Levant, who wrote numerous letters home that were passed around as literary treasures of no mean order. Not that they were very well written, but perhaps they were thought valuable as a record for posterity of the geography and history of the Levant, not to mention of Lady Hester. I suppose there is some similarity with Mrs. Danby-Davis, but I cannot see Henrietta making a pilgrimage to Jerusalem."

"Perhaps not, but presiding over a Bedouin encampment would be just her—"

"—cup of tea?"

They both laughed at that, and Celia said, "Can you not picture her brewing sassafras tea for the camel drivers?"

"Do they have sassafras in the Levant?"

"She would take it with her just to be sure—packed in the baggage that one horse could carry."

He laughed again and, from sheer high spirits, picked up a stone and threw it far into the waves. He offered her a stone of her own, but she shook her head. He tried to press it into her hand, but she pulled away. He shrugged and left her to watch his graceful movements as he threw the second stone after its fellow, seeming to enjoy the simple physical activity, perhaps as a release from the necessarily unhappy thoughts he had brought to the beach with him.

For herself, Celia did not care what they did as long as they were able to carry on this kind of nonsensical conversation, which she much preferred to his flights of gallantry. She was not accustomed to that kind of thing and did not know how to respond. However, if her heart was uncertain, there was nothing wrong with her mind, and an exchange that depended on wit challenged her.

Then it occurred to her that he might be a step ahead of her after all, and that this was the way he chose to flirt with her—flattering her with praise of her poetry, challenging her on her own ground. Possibly she ought still to consider him dangerous—unwittingly perhaps, but definitely a threat to the heart.

Unaware of being viewed as any sort of danger, Mr. Lambert wiped his hands, on his handkerchief this time, and said, "Shall we go a little farther and see what else we may find in these pools?"

He took her hand to pull her along. When she resisted, he stepped back again and pulled her fingers to his lips instead, brushing a light kiss over them as he studied her intently.

"You taste like salt," he said in a low voice.

She snatched her hand away, too dismayed now even to look at him.

"We ought to go back," she said, gathering up her wet and bedraggled skirts and glancing up to see how far they had come from where she left her horse. She reached into her pocket for her watch, but changed her mind when she realised she would have to explain it to him. "It must be late," she contented herself with saying.

He smiled. "I do beg your pardon, dear, *respectable* Mrs. Morland, for being so indiscreet as to cause you possible embarrassment. I can blame it only on the sea air and an insatiable curiosity about what . . . well, never mind that. I wonder if they have left us any breakfast. Is there a path up this side?"

"Yes, just beyond that large rock."

He found it a moment later and reached his hand out to help her up the first steep steps cut out of the rock by the wind and tides. She hesitated momentarily but told herself it was foolish to refuse his assistance when she might otherwise take an ignominious tumble, so she put her hand in his. He squeezed it reassuringly, but she could only think of how warm and strong his grasp was. She stumbled twice before they reached the top all the same.

9

DECLINING BREAKFAST, CELIA went immediately up to her room to change her sea-soaked clothing. Even then, she did not feel entirely herself, and before she washed her hands, she could not resist touching her lips to them to see if they did indeed taste of salt. They did, and she held her breath for a moment, remembering the feel of Nicky Lambert's hand holding her own so firmly. She washed her hands—scoured them—all the while telling herself that she was a fool to be so taken in by a smile and a pair of laughing eyes.

She would go away for a week, she told herself—well, for a day or two, at any rate. Surely Kitty would not do anything foolish in such a short time, but Celia was not so certain of herself. She had best go home.

Home. That was why she loved her little cottage by the sea. It was the first place she had ever been able to call her own. Kitty had never been able to understand that, although she had tried to sympathise. To Kitty home was the manor because it had everything that anyone could possibly want from life within its walls—or at least within its acres. She had not understood that part of the charm of Celia's cottage was that she had to go into the village two or three times a week to buy food and other necessities. To Celia that provided other nourishment as well and made the coming home, even after only an hour, that much more pleasant. It was the cottage that had inspired her best poetry—not just her window, but the sitting room and the kitchen midden and the flowers next to the front gate had inspired her to verse to express her feelings about her first and only home.

That was what she would do, then. She would go home, and not just to give herself a respite from her jumbled feelings about Nicky Lambert and her sense of obligation to Kitty. She needed to go home to restore that tranquillity she had always thought a constant in her nature, but which, it seemed now, was not so deeply rooted after all. When she hurried downstairs again to look for Kitty, however, Celia found that everyone had gone out to the garden for an archery contest.

"Miss Kitty's notion, I believe, madam," Jeffreys told Celia when she hesitated at the door, not eager to face the whole house party at once. "She was most set on it, and we know how she can be when she sets her heart on anything, do we not, madam?"

Celia had to smile at Jeffreys' avuncular lapse—he never spoke so of anyone but Kitty—and abandoned herself to joining the party. She went out the sun-parlour door to find that the early sunshine had grown stronger, so she paused to leave her shawl draped over one of the wicker chairs. As she walked across the lawn towards the distant garden, however, she hesitated again for quite another reason.

The garden would have been one of the wonders of the county had Hardwicke Manor been open to the public to wander about in awe. But Julian had no desire to be written up in guidebooks to Dorset's beauty spots, so he did not display the plan for his sweeping, deceptively unlandscaped acres—carefully set down in one of Sir Humphry Repton's famous red-leather-bound, illustrated books—as people with more of an eye to distinguishing themselves socially might do. Julian did, however, like to see his friends enjoying whatever part of the grounds most attracted them, and he made no objection to Kitty's occasional impulses to play croquet or even cricket in the garden. Celia doubted Kitty had ever seen the Red Book, nor would she have been impressed if she had.

The garden was separated from the park beyond by a hedge and a brick wall, the expanse of which was broken up by plantings of various kinds. An upper level, set off by decorative urns, was thick with flowers, while the lower level, reached by four wide steps, was largely lawn, with blooming shrubs along the footpaths.

The archery targets had been set up against the hedge, behind which Godfrey Danby-Davis was posted to mark down the scores and collect the shafts, while the archers stood in the middle of the lawn just below the steps. Julian was shooting when Celia came into the garden. He was expert at it, despite being handicapped by Lavinia, who stood too close by, cheering him on as if he were a racehorse. To be sure, his posture was as taut as any other highly bred hunter's, and a frown creased his broad brow, though that may have been only because he was concentrating. Kitty stood quietly to the side, holding out another arrow to him as if she were certain the one he had would misfire. Dressed in green with a great deal of braid trim and a braided ribbon confining her pale curls, she looked appropriately like Robin of Locksley's maid, Marian.

Sir Phineas and Henrietta Danby-Davis, whose husband's head popped up every now and then over the hedge to see what was going on, were conversing over the pansy beds— or, rather, Henrietta was talking and gesticulating in an animated manner while Sir Phineas nodded. Whether he did so in agreement with what she said or out of sheer inertia was difficult to determine. Signora di Lambrusco, nearly invisible in a green-and-red shawl that blended with the flowers, was stretched out on the grass in the far corner of the garden, her face raised to the sun. Nicky Lambert stood by himself under a tree, out of Julian's sight but well within Kitty's.

Celia stopped suddenly to look at him, and not simply because he could not see her doing so from where he stood. She felt a compulsion to look at him for longer than the covert glances she had stolen thus far had allowed. He had apparently changed his clothing more quickly than Celia was able to do, but she had lost all sense of time that morning and could not be sure precisely how long it had been since she last saw him. It seemed hours. It seemed, indeed, that she might well have imagined the whole episode on the beach. Almost as if she had dreamt that episode and wakened to a much less satisfactory reality, she felt a kind of sadness, as much for the loss of her previous satisfaction with life as for the loss of the dream.

Yet, simply looking at Nicky Lambert and being assured of his existence filled her with what she recognised now as the same light-hearted happiness she had felt when she first met Harry so many years before, but which she had never expected to feel again. She could scarcely credit it, but there was no other explanation—she had fallen in love with Nicky Lambert.

Appalled, she thought again of running away—at once—back to her cosy little cottage and her solitude. Obviously, she was more in need of a retreat than she had suspected. It was bad enough that Kitty had fallen under Nicky Lambert's spell. What use would Celia be to her love-stricken sister if she succumbed to the same affliction? She could not let this happen!

Kitty saw her and began waving frantically. Julian put down his bow and the arrow he had just aimed to glare at her, but Kitty paid no mind except to take advantage of the pause to prop the arrow case up within his reach and leave him to finish his shot in relative peace. Then she came to Celia and put her arm around her waist to pull her into the garden. Out of the corner of her eye, Celia saw Nicky Lambert smile at Kitty, who did not notice. Had they already had an opportunity to speak privately this morning, Celia wondered, or would she have to keep a close eye on them in anticipation of their doing so later in the day?

"Dearest, I'm so glad you're here!" Kitty exclaimed. "I had hoped to corner you at breakfast. I even came down earlier than usual to do so, but you had already gone off somewhere." She lowered her voice and added, "I breakfasted with Henrietta and Godfrey, and I must say I think someone might have warned me what that entailed."

Celia had to smile. "I'm sorry, my love, but I suppose no one thought you would be likely to come down as early as they begin their day." She allowed herself to be led to a bench beside the brick wall and continued, "I'm sorry I was not there to rescue you. Didn't Jeffreys tell you I'd gone riding?"

"Oh—well, I didn't ask," Kitty replied, sitting down on the bench and spreading her Lincoln-green skirts picturesquely around her. "Where did you go? To the cottage?"

Celia hesitated for a moment between a little lie and the risk that Kitty might ask for details if she told the truth. She compromised.

"Well, no, but I was near there and began to think that perhaps I should go back for a while," she said, then added quickly, so that she would not talk herself out of it, "Now that there are so many other people here to keep you company, my love, it does seem unnecessary for me to stop here at the manor when I could drive over from the cottage anytime."

"Oh, no!—" Kitty began but then, conscious-stricken, said, "Are you homesick, dearest Celia? I know I've been selfish to make you stay here, so do say if you would really rather go home, but . . ."

Celia ought to take advantage of this offer, however grudgingly made, but, conscious of a kind of tearing inside her, as if a connexion had been broken somewhere, she could not do it. She swallowed the heartsickness she would never be able to explain to Kitty and sighed. "But what, Kitty?"

"Oh, Celia, please stay a little longer. I do so need your help now!"

Kitty looked so earnest that Celia was concerned. "My help? But what's wrong?"

Just at that moment, however, they were interrupted by a round of applause for Julian, who had scored a bull's-eye directly on top of his previous bull's-eye, causing Godfrey Danby-Davis to gesticulate wildly from behind the hedge and Lady Proctor to give Julian a loud kiss on the cheek. He removed himself from her grasp just as Kitty ran up to give him a hug and surreptitiously rub the red mark off his cheek with her handkerchief.

"I absolutely refuse to try to follow that performance," Mr. Lambert announced as he joined Sir Phineas, who had approached Celia to bow and say good morning. She observed no trace in Nicky of their morning walk. His hazel eyes twinkled at her, however, to indicate that he remembered their earlier encounter perfectly well.

"What about you, Mrs. Morland?" he asked. "Are you expert with the bow also?"

Before Celia could reply, Sir Phineas spoke up in continuation of what seemed to have been an earlier subject of conversation between the two gentlemen. "What, are there no red Indians where you come from, young man, to teach you to use the bow and arrow? Or do they confine themselves to poisoned spears in your part of the antipodes?"

"Not at all, sir," Nicky replied politely but with a smile in his voice. "Our natives are very civilised. They carry guns. They are also in the main white, not red, and for that matter do not think of themselves as natives."

Sir Phineas chuckled, conceding the verbal contest for the moment, and asked Celia, "Will you not challenge our host's crown, dear lady? Miss Morland tells me you are a fine shot."

"I'm sure she always hits the mark," Mr. Lambert said, offering Celia his arm to escort her to the place marked off on the lawn for the archers to stand. Well, if he was with her, Celia reasoned, allowing herself to touch his sleeve lightly, he would not be off somewhere exchanging secrets with Kitty.

"You must forgive me for joining you late," she said. "Are we shooting individually or have teams been made up?"

"Nothing so formal," Nicky said. "Although I would not be averse to making a small wager on Mrs. Morland's skill. Sir Phineas, will you take me up on it?"

"You are very rash," Celia warned him, "particularly after Mr. Hardwicke's perfect score just now."

"Nearly perfect," he said. "His first shot was not even on target."

"Speaking of targets," Sir Phineas said, lowering his voice as Celia took up the bow and Mr. Lambert's challenge, "one of you may be able to clear up a little mystery. How is it, do you suppose, that the delectable Kitty came to hit on our estimable—but you must concede, unusually sober-minded—host for a husband? It has been puzzling Lady Proctor."

It had been puzzling Celia for much longer, and she paused in the act of nocking her arrow to hear Nicky's answer. But he was waiting for her to shoot, so that she was obliged to draw and aim, all the while exceedingly conscious of his eyes on her. She aimed and shot hurriedly. Naturally her arrow went wide of the mark, although it did not actually miss the target entirely, for which she supposed she ought to be grateful.

"Oh, dear," she said, with a little laugh that she hoped sounded less strained to the others than it did to her. "I fear I am out of practice. Perhaps you ought to take Mr. Lambert up on his wager, Sir Phineas."

"You only need to relax a little," Nicky said. "Try another."

Thus incited, Celia chose a second arrow, nocked it, and drew as Nicky watched her fingers closely. She was about to send up a little prayer of thanks that he found nothing wrong in her technique, but just then he reached over her shoulder and said, "A little higher, I think."

He put one hand over hers to hold the arrow where she had anchored it under her chin to aim. With the other he touched her fingers on the bow, raising them very slightly. She felt herself abnormally sensitive to his nearness and the length of his arm along hers. It was all she could do to listen to what he was saying and look at the target. Fortunately, her arrow hit the compressed straw with the kind of satisfying *thwump* that told her she had come close to the bull's-eye. She would have been satisfied at that, but Nicky was not.

"Once more."

She looked at him and saw the smiling challenge in his eyes.

"You can do it," he said. "Never settle for near-enough when you are capable of doing a thing perfectly."

So she shot again, without his help this time, and with no seeming effort she did indeed hit the bull's-eye. She smiled her satisfaction, then turned, one brow raised quizzically, for his approval.

"You see," he said, returning her smile, "I knew you could do it."

He did not, she noticed, praise her for her success, and she thought him very demanding to expect perfection as if it were nothing out of the way. Then, with a flash of insight, she realised that he made a distinction between striving to do what one could as best one could and learning a new skill, which required encouragement and words of praise along the way. That was why he encouraged Kitty in her little amusements until she had mastered them, after which he doubtless expected her to perform them perfectly, although only Kitty became impatient when she could not. Nicky, Celia somehow knew, would be a very patient teacher. She wondered if Kitty understood how fortunate she was in that.

Sir Phineas was less precise in his demands, however, and let out a "hurrah!" that nearly burst a waistcoat button and caused every head—including Signora di Lambrusco's sleepy one—to turn towards them. That made Celia and Nicky laugh and fortunately dissipated some of the electricity between them before anyone else could detect it. Celia was, therefore, almost herself when the subject that had caused her initial consternation came up again.

She stripped off her glove and handed it to Henrietta, who was to shoot next, while Celia took Sir Phineas's arm to stroll around the garden. Since Kitty was engaged in a tête-à-tête with Julian on the bench at the other side of the garden, Nicky joined them once again and replied at last to Sir Phineas's question.

"Kitty is the most loyal and affectionate of girls," he said. "She has had an understanding with Julian for years and has no intention of betraying it simply because other people may think she has chosen badly."

"Not badly, surely," Celia said, her heart contracting at the regret in his voice. If nothing else she must make him see that Kitty would be happy with Julian despite outward appearances, so that Nicky would not be hurt if Kitty could not bring herself to elope with him after all. "Simply because Julian is less—less volatile than Kitty," she went on, "does not mean that he is less—as you put it, Mr. Lambert—loyal and affectionate. Doubtless Kitty knows Julian far better than any of us do and—and loves him for qualities we cannot appreciate. I am sure they could be very happy together."

She could not feel that she had stated this with any conviction, but she glanced tentatively at Nicky to see if what she had said was any consolation. He was looking at Kitty and Julian, who had opened the gate to walk down the other side of the wall to relieve Mr. Danby-Davis's solitude. Nicky was frowning. It was then that Celia remembered Kitty's words to her. *I need you now,* she had said. But why now more than any other time? What was Celia capable of that Kitty, who had heart and courage as well as loyalty and affection, could not do for herself?

Of course. She must be having second thoughts about eloping with Nicky Lambert. Even Kitty must occasionally have attacks of conscience—or perhaps only a realisation of what she would be giving up for love of Nicky Lambert. Perhaps he was unaware of the depth of her affection for him. How could he take her seriously, after all, when Kitty flirted with him so lightheartedly, as if he were no more than a pleasant pastime? He must mean more than that to her, but Kitty simply did not know how to convince him of it or to elicit any sign of his true feelings. Celia could certainly understand that difficulty. If it were she . . .

But it was not, so Celia made up her mind there and then to put her own chaotic feelings aside. She must help Kitty. Kitty had asked her to, and in any case there was nothing Celia wanted more than to see Kitty—and Nicky Lambert, too—happy. Even it if was with each other.

10

CELIA HAD NOT intended to voice the thought, but Kitty had the same one and fewer qualms.

"I must say," she remarked, as she and Celia made themselves ready for an excursion on one of the new-fangled paddle-wheel steamers on Lyme Bay, "Julian has been particularly clever lately at devising interesting entertainments. Fancy his knowing where to hire a paddle wheeler."

Celia thought this the least curious aspect of the outing, having heard about the steamers in great mechanical detail from Harry when the first small and rather clumsy models appeared off the coast a few years before. They had since become, if not precisely a daily occurrence, at least not such an uncommon sight as to turn the heads of those Lyme residents who gathered to exchange news and conduct business in the ancient arcade of the Custom-House.

"I believe this one has a sail as well," Celia said, "and is capable of crossing the Channel."

"Good," said Kitty, taking one of her practical turns, "then no one is likely to become seasick."

"I shouldn't wager too much on Sir Phineas's constitution," Celia cautioned her. "Even if he does not suffer from mal de mer, he is perfectly capable of claiming indisposition to avoid conversation with Henrietta Danby-Davis."

The ladies laughed, as they descended the stairs to meet the rest of the party outside the front door, at Sir Phineas's recently more blatant dismay whenever the voluble Henrietta approached him. She had taken a sudden liking to Sir Phineas and followed him everywhere, impervious to hints and oblivious to his monosyllabic replies to her conversational overtures.

"Unfortunately, Lavinia finds it all highly amusing and refuses to come to his rescue," Kitty said. "It is too bad of her."

"Oh, I expect she will not let it go on for too long," Celia said.

They emerged from the house, still smiling, to find the rest of the party waiting beside the open carriage that would take them down to the Cobb at Lyme Regis, where they would board the steamboat. Celia was a little taken aback to find all four gentlemen smiling at her, and certain that their admiration was really directed at Kitty, she paused just long enough for her sister-in-law to precede her by a few steps. Kitty, of course, having utterly no self-consciousness about being looked at, made the loveliest of pictures in her red pinafore-dress with a white muslin scarf demurely outlining the square-cut bodice and another draped over her head. " . . . to keep the breeze from disturbing it," she had told Celia who had suggested that something warmer might be of more use on the water. Celia, even knowing that she looked far from dowdy herself in a new saffron-coloured walking dress with a handkerchief front and rows of embroidery at the hem, offered to carry Kitty's shawl as well as her own so as not to spoil the effect of Kitty's ensemble.

"Does she know she looks the image of Emma Hamilton as 'Nature'?" Mr. Lambert whispered to Celia as he handed the shawls up to her in the carriage. "Or is she as ignorant of the coincidence as she appears?"

He was complete to a shade himself, Celia thought, in a deceptively rustic costume of pale buff breeches and a nankeen jacket with a dark red handkerchief tied around his throat. She tore her eyes from him long enough to look at Kitty, who was standing on the edge of the grass in precisely the pose in which Mr. Romney had painted the notorious Lady Hamilton—then, of course, the less well known Miss Hart. Celia could see the justice of this remark and hesitated ever so briefly before she caught Mr. Lambert giving her a quizzical look.

"Kitty would never . . . "

He laughed. "You are caught, dear Mrs. Morland, between insulting your sister's education or her manners."

"Nonsense," Celia retorted. "You, sir, have invented my dilemma and thrust me into it. I know Kitty well enough to be certain that whether intended or not, she will take no unfair advantage of her resemblance to that other, far less innocent beauty, and that is all that matters."

He made a little bow, acknowledging the hit, but the smile that went with his unspoken apology gave Celia no satisfaction. She had not intended to sound so censorious of him by professing acceptance of Kitty's foibles.

There being room for only four in her carriage, Mr. Lambert, Mr. Hardwicke, and both Danby-Davises rode alongside. Sir Phineas held court in the carriage, where his wife, Celia, and Kitty teased him about his aversion to the idea of travelling anywhere on horseback.

"My dear Miss Morland," he rumbled. "Think of the poor horse! He should rather take an aversion to having to carry *me!*"

Their progress through the lanes to the post road and then down the steep hill to Lyme Regis was leisurely, giving Sir Phineas ample opportunity to amuse the ladies, which he was not hesitant to do, and even Lavinia laughed at stories she had doubtless heard a score of times before. This, along with the narrowness of the road, effectively prevented Mr. Lambert from pursuing his flirtation with Kitty. He was well aware of her, however, Celia could not help but notice, for whenever she looked his way herself, she caught him averting his eyes as if reluctant to be seen indulging himself in admiration of what he had claimed to consider artifice on Kitty's part.

The day's itinerary, enthusiastically if somewhat incoherently mapped out by Kitty over a late supper the night before, was to include breakfast in town before the party boarded the steamer. Accordingly, the carriage paused before the Lion Inn and allowed its passengers to alight. Julian, ever the conscientious host, bowed the ladies inside, where they made themselves at home in the parlour and enjoyed the novel sensation of being waited on by someone other than their own servants. Nicky and Kitty, of course, led the conversation, with the Danby-Davises not far behind. Ibrahim, who had come down to town an hour before to see that everything was arranged for them, stood impassively behind Sir Phineas, where he was forgotten by everyone but Kitty. She now and then glanced apprehensively up at him.

Julian, Celia thought, did not look as if he were enjoying this holiday from his duties at the manor. She wondered if he might prefer working hard at home to finding his leisure somewhere else.

"I have not had an opportunity of late to thank you," she said to him, taking advantage of having been seated beside Julian by the innkeeper's wife.

"For what?"

"For making me feel so comfortable at the manor. I daresay you put up with me only because you must, for Kitty's sake."

"Nonsense."

"Nevertheless, you have been very kind, and I quite understand now why Kitty so loves the manor. I admire the comfort I find there, as I imagine you do, but for Kitty there is so much more. Indeed, sometimes when I go to look for her, I will find her in some room I had never noticed before, where she will have found a secret cupboard or an initial carved in the panelling by some long-forgotten Hardwicke. She finds the history of the house endlessly fascinating."

Celia paused, thinking that she had perhaps let her imagination carry her away in her praise, but she could see that what she had said gratified Julian very much. He smiled. "Thank you for telling me that."

Emboldened, she added, "I also wanted to say, Julian, that you must not mind that Kitty seems to take so little interest in the actual management of the household. I think it is simply that she has so much love for and awe of the manor that she is reluctant to interfere in its workings until she is truly its mistress. It is a kind of superstition she has, I believe."

This did not meet with quite the satisfaction her first remarks had elicited, but Julian, if he did not smile, at least looked thoughtful, so Celia had to be content. She could not be entirely sure that she had accomplished anything towards a reconciliation between Julian and Kitty, but she did not care to risk meddling any further. She therefore turned the conversation by asking after those members of Julian's family with whom she was acquainted and was told that he had had a letter from his Aunt Harriet—she who had been a bosom-bow, as Kitty put it, of the Danby-Davises—warning Julian not to let them into the house under any circumstances if he wished to keep his servants and his sanity.

"Oh, dear," Celia exclaimed. "Did she really say that?"

"Absolutely," Julian assured her. "Aunt Hetty has always been outspoken. How do you suppose she came to be on terms with oddities like the Danby-Davises? But I wrote to assure her that her warning was both too late and unnecessary, since thus far I have contrived to keep both my staff and my mental equilibrium. Of course, I should have had to say that, whatever the case might be, or risk *her* descending on us as well!"

He looked at Celia, and she was glad to see he was at his ease finally, for he smiled and said, jokingly, "Of course, I may be no proper judge of that. Do I seem to you quite sound of mind?"

"Certainly more than most of us."

He gave her a look of mock horror. "Does that mean I have been living in a fool's paradise after all? What have my guests been doing behind my oblivious back?"

Celia laughed—a little artificially, she feared—but assured him that nothing at all was amiss with either his hospitality or the beneficiaries of it. He said he was relieved to hear it, and they fell to discussion of more prosaic matters having to do with the household, which set Celia once again to wondering why Kitty seemed to show no interest in them. Precisely because they were prosaic, she supposed, then gave a mental shrug. It scarcely mattered, after all, since the manor would run along quite smoothly whether Kitty held the reins or not. What really concerned her about Kitty made such concerns irrelevant in any case.

When they had at last finished their breakfast, somewhat later than Kitty's schedule allowed, everyone was eager to get to the steamer. Sir Phineas went out to the yard to bully the ostlers, and the ladies went out to the street to await their carriage. Celia glanced down the hill and thought she would as soon walk, but the Cobb was still some distance away. Besides, it would look most odd if she detached herself from the rest of the party.

She was not, it turned out, the only one to feel a certain impatience, engendered no doubt by their large breakfast and the tang of the sea air. When they had reached the bottom of Broad Street and the carriage continued its sedate progress along the seaside road known as the Walk, Mr. Lambert suddenly turned his horse down to the Cart Road, which ran along the beach, and spurred him to a canter. Letting out a whoop, Godfrey Danby-Davis and his wife followed suit, kicking up sand with the speed of their progress.

If it was a race, Celia thought, it was no contest, for Mr. Lambert was well in front the whole way to the Cobb. Indeed, he seemed unaware of being followed, as if he were racing something else. He had an oddly intent look on his handsome face, and when he did reach the stone jetty, that expression turned to an almost comic dismay when he saw both Danby-Davises bearing down on him. He glanced at the carriage again, and Celia could not help laughing even though she could not explain to Kitty—or for that matter, to herself—what made her do so. It was less that she was amused than exhilarated, as if she had been on that horse, too. The feeling shocked some deep part of her that had never before been touched—that she had not, indeed, even known existed. For a few seconds, she no longer had anything in common with the cool, sensible Celia she had thought herself to be, nor even with the warmer, romantic Celia Harry had brought out in her. She was suddenly entertaining thoughts of such abandon that all she had ever learned of love began to take on new and fascinating meanings. And all because Nicky Lambert raced down the beach on a horse.

When, a few moments later, she put her hand out to his to descend from the carriage again, she could not help noticing that his hair was still disarrayed from the wind and his eyes sparkled with the excitement that had transferred itself to her without deserting him. He gazed back at her as if he understood what she felt. She hesitated, but when he squeezed her hand lightly, it was as if a spell were broken. She let go of his hand abruptly and walked away, up the wide stone steps to the Cobb. She was at the top before she realised that she was alone and stopped there, feeling foolish. She waited for the others to catch up, and they walked out along the stone jetty to the steamboat, which appeared to be a sort of hybrid of a sailboat and one of Mr. Stevenson's locomotives.

"What a very odd looking contraption," Henrietta said. "Do you not agree, Sir Phineas?"

Sir Phineas grunted and glanced at Henrietta as if he thought the boat was nothing odd compared with her. Lady Proctor took pity on her husband and put her arm in his to be guided up the gangplank. The others followed, undeterred by their vessel's lack of beauty.

The water was unusually smooth, and no one's constitution was put to any sort of a test when the boat began to move away from the solid grey mass of the Cobb into the open bay. Kitty leaned eagerly over the railing to watch the paddle turning furiously to push them slowly forward. Julian had to pull her away, promising that she would have a better view from where the captain stood on a raised platform surveying his domain.

Kitty went off with Julian to meet the captain, leaving Celia to Sir Phineas, who had installed himself in a wooden deck chair, obviously intending to stay there for the entire voyage. They were spared unsolicited company, for the Danby-Davises were so invigorated by the sea air that they immediately set off on a brisk walk along the seaward side of the deck. On the landward side, a short distance from Celia and Sir Phineas, Nicky Lambert was playing the gallant to Lady Proctor as they leaned against the railing admiring the horizon.

Lavinia was clearly out of her element, and the bright sunlight did little to conceal the ravages of time and old scandals on her complexion even when she opened a pink parasol to shade her face from its revealing rays. Celia fancied that Nicky felt a little sorry for Lavinia and admired him for his effort to make her forget that she was no longer either pretty or youthful.

Kitty's thoughts apparently ran along the same lines, for when she and Julian rejoined them and Sir Phineas turned his deaf ear in order to speak to Julian, she whispered to Celia, "Does Sir Phineas seem older to you than Lady Proctor? He is, you know, by a dozen years or more, but I cannot see it."

"I believe it often happens that as people grow older together, they grow closer together in looks as well as in interests and understanding. You remember how your mother was always able to finish your father's sentences even when he fell ill and was unable to remember himself what he had set out to say."

"Why, yes, that's true." The notion seemed to please Kitty, and Celia had the impression that she was making a mental note of it, but for what purpose Celia could not imagine.

"What shall we be like when we are old?" Celia asked, causing Kitty to look at her with an entirely different expression.

"I must say, you do know how to dampen a person's spirits, dear *elder* sister of mine."

Celia smiled. "Well, I don't know why that should depress your spirits. You were the one who invited the Proctors on the presumption of their having aged romantically."

Kitty had the grace to look uncomfortable at that, so Celia pressed her gently for the full truth. "Dearest, I am aware you weren't really acquainted with the Proctors before you invited them to the manor."

Kitty sighed. "I might have known I would not be able to deceive you. The sad truth is that I wrote to them after I read in the *Gazette* that they had returned to England."

"But why?"

"Because I thought they would prove—inspiring."

"And you were disappointed."

Kitty was thoughtful. "Well, I was at first. I was so certain that a woman who loves deeply must retain her beauty forever. When it turned out otherwise in Lady Proctor's case, I decided that must simply be a lesson to me not to make assumptions about people without knowing them. I shall find some other way to persuade—well, to accomplish what I had intended when I invited them here. I have not given up hope that they may prove useful."

That also gave Celia food for thought. She did not welcome those thoughts because they insisted on telling her that what Kitty intended was to provide a sterling example of a runaway marriage that had succeeded despite the original scandal and the subsequent disappointments. The Proctors' marriage had survived, certainly, but not in a manner, Celia thought, that a romantic young woman like Kitty would ordinarily find admirable. That they still loved each other was apparent, but no one could claim that either love or age had made Lavinia more beautiful or Sir Phineas less absurd.

Celia smiled to herself. Nevertheless, she liked the Proctors—more, certainly, than she would have imagined before she met them. It was a pity that Kitty did not see their real virtues or that Celia did not see a way to make use of them herself.

Dear me, Celia thought. *How calculating I am become!* She glanced at Kitty to see if she too were imagining how she could put the materials at hand to best use. Kitty was indeed looking pensive, but not happily so, and Celia could not help wondering if she were considering how least painfully to bring her engagement to Julian to an end. On the other hand, perhaps she was looking for a way to break it off with Nicky Lambert . . .

No, that would be too much to hope for.

Celia's cogitations kept her awake until dinnertime. Nearly everyone else took to his or her bed when they returned to the manor from Lyme Regis, to recover from the sea air they had breathed so deeply. Thus it was that she was waiting, ready in good time for dinner, while Kitty's maid frantically dressed the younger lady in the few minutes left to them as a result of Kitty's having overslept.

"Susan, where are those pink ribbons that go with this dress?"

"I'm sure I don't know, Miss," came an exasperated voice. "Wouldn't these lavender ones do as well?"

"Don't be absurd. Of course they won't."

There followed an agitated opening and closing of drawers, and Celia sighed. Evidently, this was no time to probe Kitty for answers to the questions Celia had been asking herself all afternoon. Why had Kitty really become engaged to Julian in the first place? Had there been anything more serious than a flirtation between her and Nicholas Lambert before this? If so, why had it come to nothing when they seemed so admirably suited?

In any case, she doubted Kitty would welcome any further prying from her. On the way home from Lyme Regis after their excursion, Celia had imagined Kitty and Nicky might have the opportunity to converse secretly again if Kitty rode Henrietta's horse, which had been offered her. To prevent that, Celia expressed a desire herself to ride. Kitty was therefore relegated to the carriage again, and Celia rode alongside Julian all the way home, doubtless causing some bewilderment on the part of the gentlemen as well as resentment from Kitty.

Well, that was too bad. At the time, Celia had felt compelled to act as she did. She may have been concerned for no cause, but she could not very well apologise to Kitty without making a piece of work of it. She would just have to hope that Kitty would put the incident out of her mind.

Restless, Celia rose from her chair and began picking up the debris left by Kitty's hasty search through her belongings for new trimmings to wear with her favourite old pink gown.

A lone white glove lay on the writing table, and as Celia reached for it and glanced around for its mate, she saw something else white on the floor and bent to retrieve that as well. It was a scrap of paper, part of a letter or some other kind of note. Celia had begun to crumple the page, reluctant to read it, when a phrase caught her eye. She glanced quickly, apprehensively, at it, and was punished for doing so as the phrase burned itself into her memory.

Let me live with you, and be your love, it read, *in our castle by the sea.*

Nicky had talked that way about his home on the sea, Celia remembered, as if it were a magic place, a scene from a fairy story.

It had never troubled Celia before that no one, not even Harry, had ever talked about fairy stories and castles in the same breath as her name. But now an unaccountable lump rose in her throat, as if all the sadness of things that could never be had concentrated itself in her. She could not be jealous of Kitty for loving Nicky Lambert. Celia could understand that too well. But why did she have to be a witness to it?

=11=

"May I come in, Julian?"

Startled by the voice when he had not heard the knock, Julian spoke before he thought.

"Yes, of course, Nicky."

Julian was a little sorry then to have his train of thought interrupted even by his friend, and the next instant was sorry again for his unintended inhospitality. But as usual, Nicky read Julian's thoughts as if he had spoken them aloud.

"Whatever you do, Julian," Nicky said, looking around for another candle to lighten the gloom Julian had, literally and metaphorically, been sitting in, "please do not apologise for my interrupting you!"

Julian laughed. "I'm sorry. Well, there you are. I must be sorry for something, it seems. I trust my ungraciousness is not so apparent to my other guests."

"You conceal it admirably. Of course, it may simply be that I am the only one ungracious enough to mention it."

"No, Kitty has even fewer qualms about telling me when I am being selfish."

"Surely, she never called you selfish."

"Well, no, her usual word is preoccupied, as in 'Julian, dear, I hope you are not too preoccupied to give me an archery lesson.'"

"I did have a reason for barging in on your—er—preoccupation like this, however," Mr. Lambert said, disposing himself gracefully in a wing chair. "Why are you being preoccupied in the dark, by the way?"

Julian did not answer, assuming the question to be rhetorical, and instead watched Nicky for a moment. He couldn't help admiring the way his clothes never seemed to mind Nicky's thoughtless treatment of them, as now, when he draped one leg over the other and leaned both elbows into the arms of the chair. Julian fell to speculating on whether Nicky had the only good tailor in the West Indies or if absolutely anything he put on his back would flatter him.

He did remember to offer Nicky a brandy, however, which was accepted. Since a decanter was always kept at hand in the library, Julian rose to pour out a glass from which Nicky took a liberal swallow. Julian grimaced.

"My dear fellow, I am grateful Jeffreys did not see that exhibition. My best brandy!"

Nicky looked up with interest. "Smuggled?"

Julian laughed. "No, it's been some time since that was necessary, you know. My sources of supply in France have long since been reestablished, and I have been blessed with several cases of very fine old brandy that had been languishing in chateaux cellars during the war."

"Well, I beg your pardon for not showing it the proper respect. I'm afraid I have become too used to rum and other much less exalted potations."

"I shall send you regular reminders, in that case, of the advantages of the old world."

"Thank you," Nicky said, taking a more sedate sip of the brandy.

"See here, Nicky," Julian said, seating himself again. "Are you happy in Jamaica? Do you never think of coming home to settle?"

A slight frown creased Nicky's wide forehead, and it was a moment before he said, "I've thought of it, but there is—there has not been anything to come back for. I have a very comfortable life at Indigo Hill and more land than I could ever own here, which brings me a tidy profit every quarter. I like the people there. Those who work for me seem to be content. God knows, the climate is a vast improvement over England's."

He sounded, Julian thought, as if he were enumerating the virtues of his home in order to persuade himself of them. Nicky had done the same thing in his first letters to England after settling there. After a year those letters had become less frequent, and their tone had changed, indicating that Nicky had begun to settle in nicely. That hadn't surprised Julian particularly. Nicky had always had the devil's own knack for landing on his feet after every adversity and of turning disaster into prosperity with no visible effort. Intelligence helped, of course, and optimism tempered with a careful analysis of the opportunities presented him before he took them up, but it was Nicky's luck that Julian had always envied.

Nevertheless, it seemed that there was something missing in the rosy picture he painted, or something he had not previously known he missed. Julian wondered if he ought to pry, or simply let Nicky tell him in his own good time.

"Perhaps I'll bring the first shipment to you myself," Julian said. "I must admit to a certain curiosity about this plantation of yours. Shall I be obliged to sleep on a straw mat and eat coconuts?"

Nicky smiled. "Only if you really wish to. I should recommend the bed, however, and the native fish. We'll even cook it for you."

Julian laughed. "You needn't try to bamboozle me as I heard you do to Sir Phineas. I assure you, I am not so ignorant about the Indies as to suppose you eat your fish raw."

"Oh, but Phineas believed that because, it seems, in the Orient and some other unusually foreign spots he has travelled to, it really is common to eat raw fish. In fact, I've given up trying to gammon him, for he really is awake on all suits and only goes along with my jest when it strikes his fancy to do so. But, look, Julian—that reminds me of what I wanted to say to you. I had a chat with Lady Proctor on the ship this afternoon."

"I noticed," Julian said, smiling. "And I am ever in your debt for whatever you said to her to make her so amenable to every amusement offered her."

"Only a variation on the common or garden variety of Canterbury tale that Kitty has heard a dozen times. I hesitated to try it on Mrs. Morland, however, so I approached Lady Proctor instead."

"Speaking of Mrs. Morland—"

"No, let us not just yet, if you don't mind."

Julian raised an eyebrow. So that was it. He had been right not to pry, judging by Nicky's touchy reaction to the slightest probe, so for now Julian conceded with a shrug to his earnest request. He had an idea that Nicky had taken more than just a passing fancy to Celia, but he also suspected that his feelings were at a delicate stage just now and any advice even his best friend offered could bruise them. Julian could be patient about that.

He was, however, finding himself increasingly and uncharacteristically impatient about the progress of his own relationship with Kitty. That he had taken his time about making up his mind to marry her did not lessen that impatience, and that Kitty seemed to accept his doubts as something of no importance which he would sort out for himself only made him more self-critical. Kitty had a remarkable gift for soothing his doubts and nursing his touchy pride, but even she could not be so tolerant forever. Especially not at nineteen.

Julian wondered if she had ever really considered what life with him would be like. It was not that he could not make her comfortable, and he would certainly do his best to make her feel loved. However, that was not something natural to him as it was to Kitty, and he knew that the effort would sometimes be beyond him. There was always the risk that he would hurt her without intending to. On the other hand, he had never really considered what life without Kitty would be like. He was, admittedly, inclined to take things for granted, but he knew it would be fatal to treat Kitty so. He must never stop fighting for her.

"I take it, then," he said to Nicky, "that you wanted to report something that Lavinia said to you?"

"It was something she showed me, actually. I could not think of a plausible excuse to borrow it, unfortunately, so I leave it to you to contrive a way of looking for yourself. It was a locket with a portrait inside of Sir Phineas as a young man."

"And?"

"And—now this is a very curious thing—he was the very image of a man I once knew hereabouts. Mind you, it's been years since I last saw Lucas and my memory . . . what's the matter?"

Julian was unaware of having moved forward suddenly at Nicky's words, but he must have done so because Nicky leaned back ever so slightly in his own chair as if he were about to be attacked by a large and unfamiliar dog. Julian was certainly holding his breath. He let it go and made an effort to calm himself.

"Who is this man?"

"A farmer by the name of Lucas Tyler. As I say, I haven't seen him for years, and he may no longer live in the district."

"Local farmers tend to stay put, I'm afraid."

Nicky frowned. "Why *afraid*, Julian?"

Julian hesitated. He had not wanted to reveal his fears to anyone, perhaps because that would give them substance and, thus, a truth he had fought against. But he had never been reluctant to confide in Nicky before. Julian trusted him, and now he must show that trust by speaking of this thing that he so feared.

"There is a possibility that I am not the true master of Hardwicke Manor."

Nicky gave a low whistle. "But how could that be?"

Julian attempted to marshall his thoughts. His previous

certainty about his future had received a considerable jolt with Nicky's news, and Julian was uncertain now how to explain himself. He went back to the beginning.

"As you know, Lady Proctor was my father's first wife."

"Before she eloped with Phineas. Yes, my father drilled the story into me when I was at an age to take it as a cautionary fable. I have had the devil of a time getting over that."

Julian smiled reluctantly. "Yes, it's difficult not to like them despite the scandal, isn't it? And I must confess to some sympathy for what Lady Proctor must have endured from my father. He was never the most affectionate of men."

Nicky smiled. "I never knew him well, myself. I only remember that as a boy I was never eager to come to the manor and have to pass his scrutiny—invariably with soiled stockings or a torn sleeve—while I waited to see you. When you came to us, I could always tell if you had just been given an improving homily because your mood would be as black as pitch, and it was a labour of Hercules to charm you out of it."

"I'm sorry. I never realised I was so difficult a friend."

"You weren't—except for this continuing impulse to apologise for yourself. I knew it was partly to do with your being an only child. I had so many older brothers and sisters to beat any sensitivity to criticism out of me that I was never offended by your moods. I suppose I looked on them as a lack you could not help—having a large family, I mean. That's why I kept offering you mine."

Julian had to laugh. "Here I thought you pitied me for being lonely."

"It just goes to show how friendships are built on the most unlikely misunderstandings, doesn't it? But look, Julian, what do the Proctors' past sins have to do with your inheritance? Lavinia has no children."

"So I had always believed. But recently I came upon my father's diary for the years of their marriage. Lavinia was indeed brought to bed of a son whom she believes to have died at birth."

"But he did not?"

"I do not believe so. I have made discreet enquiries, but I have been unable to find a record of the boy's birth, much less his death. It does not seem that he was baptised in a local church, and he was certainly not buried here. There is no trace of a grave in the parish churchyard or even in the neighbouring parishes."

"You seem to have made a thorough investigation."

"So I thought. You may have noticed my slipping away for a ride several times this past week. I also hired an agent with no connexion to the family to make enquiries further afield than I could go without arousing attention. The one thing that never occurred to me to investigate, however, which ought perhaps to have been the first, is what you have just reminded me of."

"You mean . . . the boy may have been Phineas's?"

"Precisely. That would account for my father's not acknowledging the child's existence. But it also makes it more likely that the child is alive somewhere, possibly unaware of his true ancestry."

"But if he were alive, he would not be a threat to you. Not if he was not your father's son. And if he is unaware of his history, he will not even consider it."

"Nevertheless I must be certain. I must see the man for myself and, if necessary, secure his written pledge that he will make no claim on the manor in future. I do not wish to be hard, but I have come to the point where I must be. When did you last see this man Lucas Tyler? The name means nothing to me."

"That's scarcely surprising. He lived on a farm on the other side of our land from the manor and thus some distance removed from you. The Tylers, as I recall, always did their marketing and other business in Axminster rather than Lyme or Charmouth. Come to think on it, that always struck me as odd, as if they were deliberately avoiding any contact with the manor. In any case, I have not seen Lucas for at least three years, not since I was last in England."

"But he may still live here."

"Look, Julian—what does it matter? Presumably your father recognised the boy's ancestry at his birth and sent him to be raised by the Tylers, under what conditions we do not know. But they have never applied to you for anything, have they? Your father either paid them well, or they did not know where their foundling came from. Why not let sleeping dogs lie?"

"I must know the truth," Julian insisted. "For Kitty's sake."

"Kitty?" Nicky's tone revealed his disbelief. "Surely it matters even less to her. It is you she loves, Julian, not Hardwicke Manor."

"Perhaps you do not know Kitty as well as you think, Nicky."

"Are you trying to tell me she agreed to marry you only to be lady of the manor? As little as you think I know her, Julian, I am certain that at least is untrue, and even without being told it, I am certain she has told you a hundred times that she loves you if she has said it once."

It was true enough. Julian knew he ought to believe it, but he had never been able to accept Kitty's love fully and he could not now answer Nicky's accusation.

"Then it is for my sake that I must be certain. I must find this Lucas Tyler and set my own mind at ease that I am offering Kitty—along with my unworthy self—a home and a future that will be worthy of her."

Nicky sighed. "Very well. I was never one to dispute the sincerity of self-interest, and I refer not only to yours, by the way. I shall be delighted to see you and Kitty thoroughly married as soon as possible, if only because that alone will convince Mrs. Morland that you two are meant for each other and no one else."

"Who else does she imagine is involved?"

Nicky gave a rueful laugh. "My dear fellow, you would never believe it. I will tell you all about it after I have convinced you that Kitty loves you despite every obstacle you insist on erecting in her way. Although I am beginning to see that it might be easier to remove the obstacles. Have you a lance?"

"A what?"

"A lance, such as knights go to battle dragons with. You have any number of suits of armour around the place. Surely we can come up with the appropriate accoutrements. When can we start?"

"Start? Oh, on our quest, you mean," Julian said, despite himself getting into the spirit of Nicky's absurd jest. "I must speak to Lavinia first. Then we may—well, go directly to the dragon's lair, I suppose."

"Known to its more prosaic neighbours as the Tyler Farm?"

"The very place." Julian stood up to pull the bell and, when Jeffreys responded, asked to beg a few minutes of Lady Proctor's time as soon as she might come to him.

"Perhaps you will see to our horses, Nicky."

"Not yet. There's no telling how long we will be with Lavinia. Yes, *we*, Julian. I would not miss this interview for the world!"

12

THE NEXT PERSON to enter the library was not Lady Proctor, however, but Kitty, who knocked tentatively before putting her head inside the door to be greeted with two hopeful, then crestfallen, faces.

"Julian—? Oh, I'm sorry." Faltering, she made as if to back out again, murmuring, "I thought you were alone. I mean . . ."

Nicky laughed, but when Kitty reddened and lowered her eyes, Julian stifled his own impulse to tease her about her wanton desire to be alone with him and gently invited her to come in.

Encouraged by his smile, she closed the door softly behind her and seated herself on the arm of his chair. Out of the corner of his eye, Julian could see Nicky raise his eyebrows at him quizzically, but Julian thought he could contrive to be both dignified and kind to Kitty at the same time. He was soon to be disillusioned.

"Julian . . . ," Kitty began in that cajoling way he had come to recognise and almost to enjoy—except when there was a witness to it. Being observed diminished the charm of these little intimacies for him, even if it did not deter Kitty. When she ran her finger down his waistcoat front, therefore, Julian could feel himself begin to fidget.

"Julian, may we give a dinner party next week?"

"It seems to me, Kitty, that we have a party for dinner every night."

"Oh, you know what I mean. A proper party, with music

and dancing afterwards. Not that I mean we should invite a great many people—only perhaps another dozen or so. Perhaps twenty, from the neighbourhood. I know that Maria and Eva Singleton at Northridge are forever complaining that there is not a sociable evening to be had more than once a month in this season."

"And what is the occasion, that we must entertain the Singleton girls?"

Kitty looked up at Julian from beneath a fine veil of lashes and said nothing for a moment, then shrugged lightly. "Oh . . . no occasion. I just thought you might like to do it."

"Well, since most of the burden of the preparations will fall on Jeffreys and Mrs. Milsom, I would naturally enjoy it. Will you choose a date and make up a guest list and address the invitations?"

"Oh, yes! Indeed, I have a list already. Shall I bring it to show you?"

She jumped up as if she would run off and get the list at once, and Julian was obliged to frustrate her.

"I'm sorry, Kitty, but not just now. We'll talk of it in the morning, shall we? We are expecting—that is, I must take care of some estate business now."

"Now?" Kitty repeated. "Aren't you going to come down to supper and listen to Celia read afterwards? We've gone back to *Ivanhoe*, and we're just at the part where—"

"Yes, I'll come down later," Julian assured her, laughing and pretending to push her away, "if only you'll be a darling now, Kitty, and go away. The sooner I finish my work, the sooner I'll be able to join you."

"Very well." Kitty rose, then glanced coquettishly at Nicky. "Will you come too, Nicky?"

"Of course," he said, smiling.

"Well, good-bye then—for now." Julian rose to open the door for her, and she smiled up at him as she floated gracefully out. Julian closed the door, took a deep breath, and looked at Nicky.

"In heaven's name," he said, only half in jest, "tell me

what occasion I've forgotten!"

Nicky shrugged. "My dear fellow, if you don't remember it, I certainly won't."

"What's the date today?"

"The sixth."

Julian slapped the side of the desk as he sat down again. "Damnation! I remember now. It's the day she proposed."

"Proposed what?"

"Marriage, idiot."

Nicky laughed. "Kitty proposed to *you*?"

"Do you doubt it?"

"Not at all, but you never told me."

Julian smiled ruefully. "It isn't the sort of thing a man cares to admit. I can't even say I would have done it myself eventually anyway. The truth is, it never occurred to me that she might want me."

"You're not sorry you said yes?"

"Of course not."

"Then it doesn't matter, does it, who did the asking? When was this, by the way?"

"The day Kitty came home from Bath." Julian's smile faded. "Two years ago."

Nicky seemed to understand, although he shook his head in exaggerated remonstration. "Yes, dear boy, you had better not put this marriage off too much longer."

"I won't," Julian replied grimly, "if tonight doesn't put it off altogether."

"Don't talk like that," Nicky began, and would have said something else, but at that moment there was another, much more forceful knock at the door. He smiled.

"I'll hazard a guess that Phineas has come along to protect his lady from your browbeating," he said.

"Nonsense," Julian snapped, no longer in any mood for levity. "I have no intention of browbeating anyone."

"Pardon me," Nicky retorted, "but you have resumed your headmaster's tone and are likely to do just that. Stop frowning."

Julian paused, took a deep breath, and opened the door

with a false smile that made his friend give an exasperated sigh and turn to the door himself as Sir Phineas entered warily, glancing around as if to scout the enemy's territory before gesturing Lady Proctor to come in. Nicky bowed to Phineas and smiled warmly at Lavinia. Julian recovered enough to be grateful that Nicky also raised Lavinia's hand to his lips and gave her a reassuring little wink. The gesture made her giggle and seemed to put Sir Phineas more at his ease as well.

"Trust you don't mind my comin' along, dear boy," Sir Phineas said, shaking Julian's hand. "My Lavinia wasn't feelin' quite the thing this evening, and I don't want her excitin' herself. You know how it is."

"Certainly, sir. I won't keep you a moment. Won't you sit down? A brandy, perhaps?"

Sir Phineas declined, but Lavinia's tentatively raised fingers gave Julian to understand that she would not object to a small restorative. He turned his back for a moment to pour a little brandy into a ratafia glass for her.

When they were all comfortably seated, Julian, realising that Nicky's behaviour was the best model he could follow with Lady Proctor, smiled again, genuinely this time, and leaned forward to speak confidentially to her.

"Lady Proctor—Lavinia—you must forgive me for raising this painful subject once again, but I must ask you some few further questions about—about the son you lost."

Lavinia's hands clutched her ratafia glass possessively, and her voice quavered slightly. Nonetheless, her gaze was steady as she returned Julian's and said, "What do you want to know?"

"Did you never see the child at all?"

She shook her head. "No, James took the baby away as soon as the doctor showed it to him. I suppose—well, I afterwards thought he must have been already dead, and James did not want me to see him. I was quite ill for a few days, you see."

"Did the doctor tell you the child had been stillborn?"

"Yes—no, not at the time. He did after, when I was feeling a little stronger. I don't remember very clearly what happened just after the birth."

"Was there anyone else in the room with you—a wet-nurse, or a maid?"

"Yes, there was my old nanny, but she annoyed the doctor so with her chatter that he sent her away."

"So she did not see the child either?"

Lavinia shook her head. Julian sighed. As he had suspected it would before he began, his questioning left him with no other way to find out what he needed but to ask her directly. He glanced out of the corner of his eye at Sir Phineas, who appeared to have fallen asleep in his chair, his hands, holding his handkerchief, folded over his ample stomach.

"Lavinia," Julian said, very softly. "Was James the father of that child?"

As he had guessed, Phineas was not really asleep, for he jerked himself upright at that, sputtering and waving his handkerchief agitatedly.

"How dare you, sir! You insult my wife with such a question! I—"

He closed his mouth suddenly at a sign from Lavinia and, bemused, settled back into his chair to stare at her.

"It's all right, Phineas. It is only the truth."

"But he is implying—"

Lavinia nodded. "Yes, that it was *your* child, Phineas. It was." Julian thought she was relieved to have said that after all those years.

"But—" Still unable to accept the idea, Phineas continued to stare at his wife until she gave him an indulgent smile.

"I told you, dearest, that James and I had not"—her expression was a mixture of coquetry and shyness, and Julian thought he detected a real blush beneath the rouge—"that is, we had not been husband and wife for some time."

"Yes, but—dash it all, Lavinia, I wasn't counting, and I daresay James wasn't either. He wouldn't ever have known, unless . . ."

He and Lavinia turned as one to Julian. He could see the new question rise in her eyes. He nodded.

"It is my belief that James recognised the infant's resemblance to his natural father," he told them. "Perhaps he had his suspicions before and was only waiting to have them confirmed. That is why he did not wish you to see your child."

"Then, that must also be why James was so—I mean, why he treated me so indifferently afterwards," Lavinia said. "It was that which made me run away with Phineas, you know, not because"—Lavinia glanced around, as if to reassure herself she was among friends, and the three sympathetic faces seemed to reassure her—"not because we had been lovers. We were not ashamed of that."

Lavinia lowered her eyes, but Julian saw Nicky smile and mouth the word "Brava!" as Phineas rose ponderously to his feet and moved to the back of Lavinia's chair to pat her on the shoulder.

"That's true, my dear, perfectly true. But it is good to hear you say so, just the same. I must tell you now, in turn, that I believed all along that the child was mine, but you know I would not have hurt you by speaking of it—particularly since we were never able to have another."

Lavinia smiled up at him. "It doesn't matter, does it? Haven't we been perfectly happy with only each other all these years?"

"All the same," Phineas insisted, "I should not have dragged you all over the map the way I did. You ought to have had a proper home, not just those paltry rented lodgings. We might have adopted children."

"Now, Phineas, you know I have adored every minute of it. I never missed having a house of my own. Why should I, indeed, when we have lived in rajahs' palaces and the governor's guesthouse and—do you remember that lovely houseboat in Kashmir? We've always had all the servants anyone could possibly need and, indeed, every other comfort in life."

Phineas smiled reminiscently. "Ah, yes, I remember that houseboat . . . Look here, Lavinia, have you really been happy?"

"Of course, dearest. I had you."

There was an awkward silence—or at least, so Julian felt it to be—until the elderly lovers remembered that they were not alone in the room. Sir Phineas straightened up and cleared his throat before addressing him again.

"Look here, boy—how can you be certain of all this? Have you any proof of what you say?"

"I am not at all certain, sir. I am endeavouring to uncover that proof, and I believe I am close to it."

"Close to it?" Lavinia looked puzzled. "Is there something else, Julian? Something that has happened more recently?"

He hesitated and glanced at Nicky, who also looked thoughtful for a moment, then shrugged as if to say there would never be a better time to speak of all this, if it must be spoken of.

"Lavinia," Julian said. "It is possible that your son is—that he did not die at birth."

"How can that be?"

"Are you wearing your locket, the one you showed Nicky on the boat this morning?"

Lavinia reached inside her lace fichu and drew out the locket. Phineas unfastened the clasp and handed the necklace to his wife, who passed it to Julian without looking at it.

He opened it and, trying not to seem too surprised at the handsome face that looked up at him, said, "This is a portrait of Sir Phineas as a young man?"

Lavinia smiled fondly. "Yes. Phineas gave it me as a kind of betrothal pledge, since we could not, as you know, be married at once. It is very like him, too, although no one ever believes he was so good-looking. Portraits are often flattering, but this one is very accurate."

"You see," Julian went on, "Mr. Lambert knew a man who very much resembled this portrait—a local farmer by the name of Lucas Tyler."

Lavinia took the locket back, frowning. "I don't understand."

"I believe he may be your son."

"But how can that be?"

"I believe your son did not die, but rather that James told you he did so that you would not want to see him. Then he sent the infant away to be raised by the Tylers."

"Why the Tylers, do you suppose?" Nicky asked, interrupting for the first time the interview he had been listening to in fascination for half an hour.

Julian turned to Lavinia. "Did you know the family?" he asked. When she shook her head, he looked to Nicky again and said, "That may be one reason."

"Now see here, young man," Phineas demanded, becoming increasingly agitated, "is my—our—son alive or not? We must know!"

Lavinia put up her hand to touch her husband's, and shook her head.

"Eh? What do you mean, Lavinia? Don't you want to see him?"

"I—I am not certain, Phineas. If he believes himself to be the son of these Tylers, and if his life is a happy one, would it not be best to leave him in that happiness?"

"But, Lavinia, he is your son!"

"No, dearest, he is the Tylers' son now. They would, I have no doubt, be devastated to lose him—even to be threatened with such a loss—and it is not as if we lack anything. We have long since accepted our childless state, have we not? Have we not just agreed that we have been perfectly happy with only each other?"

Phineas did not answer immediately, apparently overcome once again by sentiment, but at last he gave Lavinia's hand a kiss and said to Julian, "Well, then, my boy, I leave it to you to discover what you can. You will come to see me when you return?"

"Of course, sir."

Phineas nodded. "Good, good. Then we—I shall relay your news to Lavinia. You need not trouble yourself with that."

Understanding that he was being dismissed, Julian rose to shake Sir Phineas's hand and assure him that he would be off first thing in the morning for the Tyler Farm and would report to him immediately on his return. Then Julian kissed Lavinia's hand and smiled reassuringly at her. Nicky repeated the gesture, and a moment later they closed the door once again on Sir Phineas comforting his wife in that clumsy, but marvelously effective way Julian was beginning to wish he could emulate.

13

CELIA HAD THE distinct impression that something was happening at the manor in which she had no part. It was not so much that anyone was keeping anything from her, she thought, but that everyone else was distracted by something that did not affect her and about which no one thought to enlighten her.

The night after their excursion on Lyme Bay, when all the manor guests ought in justice to have been exhausted enough for an early bed, Celia appeared to be the only one to fall asleep, only to be awakened several times in the night by voices in the hall and footsteps on the stairs. She knew she ought not be vulgarly curious about other people's business, but Kitty at least was her friend and Celia wished she could help her—as indeed Kitty had not very long ago requested of her. Therefore, Celia rose the next morning and went downstairs early, determined to occupy the breakfast parlour until all the other guests had put in an appearance to explain themselves—by their demeanour if not by their words.

The Danby-Davises were, as usual, the first to bestir themselves. When Celia entered the room, Henrietta was humming to herself as she placed an herbal mixture in a teapot, then poured hot water over it.

"Good morning, my dear!" she chirped at Celia, banging the pot lid closed. Henrietta was dressed in a sort of shepherdess's costume, as if from a Watteau painting, complete with broad-brimmed hat and pinafore. Celia dared not speculate what occasioned such a costume. She was all too aware that it might be Henrietta's customary morning attire and she might insult her by enquiring about it.

"Good morning," she said simply. "I am glad to see you well, as always."

"Godfrey!" Henrietta called out, "What are you doing out there, dear?"

"Nothing," came a muffled voice from outside the opened French windows leading to the garden. "Only standing on my head."

"Do get off it, dear, and come to breakfast."

Celia tried not to laugh and busied herself pouring a cup of coffee. A moment later, Mr. Danby-Davis appeared, looking a trifle flushed but otherwise none the worse for his experience, and dressed, Celia was relieved to see, in conventional, if slightly rumpled, morning attire. She was thus able to enquire calmly if he had slept well and to ascertain thereby that she was not, after all, the only unenlightened member of the household.

"Splendidly, yes, thank you," Godfrey exclaimed, taking a deep breath. "What's that you have there, ma'am? Coffee, is it? Dear me. Well, to each his own, eh? Will you try some of our tea? Henny, give Mrs. Morland a cup of sassafras."

Celia dared not refuse, and the coffee had gone cold in any case. She suspected the servants of not wishing to intrude with a fresh pot where it would not be welcome. She sipped at the brew Henrietta handed her instead and was surprised to find it not uninvigorating. At least it was hot.

"Did you sleep well, Mrs.—Henrietta?" she asked.

"Oh, yes, my dear. Well, we always do, don't we, Godfrey?"

So much for their having heard anything in the night, Celia thought. Then Godfrey said something that he did not realise was revealing.

"That's right, Henny. But you know that I believe it is from my habit of reading for half an hour before retiring. Always from the best authors, naturally. Last night, I read from Mrs. Edgeworth's *Patronage*, which Miss Morland was good enough to lend me. Indeed, I met her in the hall as we were both on our way to the library, she to return a book and I to borrow one. Well, she obligingly gave me hers, and I was spared having to make a choice. I had my full half hour's read and slept like a babe."

"I had no idea Miss Morland had such elevated literary tastes," said Henrietta, a sentiment Celia would have echoed except that Mrs. Danby-Davis meant it sincerely. "I wonder if she has read *Leonora*? I could lend her my copy."

"I expect she has a copy," Celia said, to save Kitty from having to discuss the works of Mrs. Edgeworth, which appealed not at all to her taste for mediaeval romances. "I am sure I have seen it in Mr. Hardwicke's library, at any rate."

And Mr. Hardwicke's library was only a few doors away from Mr. Lambert's room, Celia recalled. Kitty must have been on her way there and had taken along the first book that came to hand. That way, if she were observed, she could claim to be on her way to the library.

"Ah, but here she is now!" Godfrey exclaimed as Kitty herself appeared in the doorway.

Kitty was dressed in a new yellow carriage dress with a design of daisies in the hem, looking—Celia thought, her mind already formulating a full-blown plot such as Mrs. Edgeworth would never have dreamed of—as if she were expecting to be driven somewhere that morning.

Kitty was—Celia could not help noticing this despite its not fitting neatly into her plot—decidedly not eager to greet the morning. She put her hand up to shield her eyes from the light coming in the windows Mr. Danby-Davis had left open and seated herself to pour a shaky cup of coffee with a caution that indicated her eyes were not quite open. It was obvious from her reddened eyes that she had been up most of the night. Her voice was certainly one of those Celia had heard in the night, now she thought on it.

"Do have a cup of sassafras tea with us," Henrietta suggested brightly. "I daresay you will find it more efficacious than that dreadful coffee for removing those shadows from under your eyes."

"How kind of you to mention them," Kitty said in a waspish tone so unlike her that Celia was sure it boded no good. Kitty took the cup of tea out of Henrietta's hand, then put it deliberately to one side and picked up her coffee again.

"Well, Kitty, if you really prefer cold coffee," Celia said, intercepting the tea before Kitty actually elbowed it off the table, "I will take this from you. I daresay Henrietta will show you how to make it after you've had something to eat, so that you may have some later. Do you shred the root to make the tea, Henrietta? I don't imagine one can use it whole, can one?"

Henrietta was happy to be distracted into a lecture on the making of herbal teas, in which Celia tried to appear interested despite her far greater preoccupation with wondering what ailed Kitty. She had picked up a plate and was uncovering the dishes on the sideboard one by one and helping herself to a teaspoonful of everything she found in them, even though, as Celia knew perfectly well, she never ate anything more than some toast and occasionally a boiled egg for breakfast. She had set all the covers down again with a clatter and little regard to whether they were placed evenly over the food they were meant to protect, when Sir Phineas strolled into the room and gave them all a jovial good morning. Kitty smiled. Celia breathed a sigh of relief.

"Sir Phineas," Kitty said, giving him a light hug with the arm that was not holding her plate. "How are you this morning?"

"Very well indeed, my dear, thank you," the old knight replied, eyeing her plate. "And ravenous! Are those kidneys I see there?"

Kitty handed him the plate. "For you, sir. I knew you would like to try a little of everything. Do you care for coffee?" she added, steering him towards the table and forestalling Henrietta's tea by picking up the coffee pot and smiling encouragingly at Sir Phineas. "Oh, dear," she said then. "I'm afraid it's gone cold. I'll ring for more, shall I?"

"Eh? Oh, thank you, my dear. But what about you? I must not take your breakfast."

"Not at all. I only wanted some toast and perhaps a boiled egg."

So saying, Kitty took another plate and went down the sideboard again in much more her usual manner. Celia breathed another sigh of relief and began to wonder if she ought to curb her imagination. It was certainly not an aid to digestion of which the Danby-Davises would approve.

The rest of the meal went along pleasantly enough, thanks largely to Sir Phineas's remarkably cheerful mood, which soon had the ladies—not excepting Henrietta—laughing at his outrageous stories. Those present were the extent of his audience, however, for Lady Proctor did not join them—Sir Phineas explaining without elaboration that she had gone to bed late the night before. Neither did Mr. Lambert nor Mr. Hardwicke put in an appearance.

"Where is Julian this morning?" Celia asked Kitty, hoping that the answer would include Mr. Lambert, but she was taken aback when Kitty's scowl suddenly reappeared and she answered curtly, "He said he would have his breakfast in his room. He and Nicky are going for a ride this morning. He wouldn't tell me where."

Astonished, Celia made no immediate response, but Sir Phineas did. Celia once again had the impression of being left out of something when he patted Kitty's hand reassuringly and said the gentlemen would doubtless be back soon and would she care to take a stroll in the garden with him in the meanwhile? Oddly enough, this suggestion seemed to please Kitty. When Sir Phineas extended it to Celia, however, she declined, having suddenly made up her mind to do something else just then. At once, in fact.

"Thank you, sir, but if you will forgive me, I have quite forgot that I was—that I promised to walk over to Mrs. Williams's cottage this morning." Celia rose and, to disguise her sudden eagerness to be quit of the room and all of its inhabitants, babbled on, "She is the lady who looks after my cottage when I am not there, you know, and she always expect news of the manor in exchange, so since I have not seen her for three days, I daresay my window boxes are in dreadful order. Do forgive me. Good morning."

So saying, she fled the room and, not even pausing for a shawl or bonnet, left the house by the kitchen door and made directly for the stables. She was afraid she had missed them, but she arrived in good time after all to find Nicky Lambert, dressed for a ride and talking to the groom who was saddling his horse. Suddenly Celia could not remember why she had been so eager to speak to him. She made a move to go away again, but the groom saw her and nodded in her direction. Nicky turned around and smiled. She could not have moved then even had she really wanted to.

"Good morning," he said, coming towards her with that wonderful smile that never failed to turn her heart over. She had to steel herself to resist its full effect and, seeing out of the corner of her eye that the groom had discreetly left them alone, to maintain her composure even as he moved closer to her.

"Good morning, Mr. Lambert."

He lowered his hands, which had reached for hers, and frowned. "What's the matter?"

"We missed you at breakfast."

He laughed ruefully. "And I missed breakfast! Julian insisted on getting away early, and now he's not even here. I don't doubt he's in the kitchen stashing away a roll and jam while I starve. I don't suppose you have a sausage or two on your person?"

Her failure even to smile at his joke brought home to him that she really was concerned about something. When she had some difficulty putting it to words, he smiled again.

"You are so rarely discomposed. You have no notion how delightful it is to watch you at a loss for words," he said, reaching his hands out again, not to take hers but to pull her gently towards him by the shoulders. She stiffened.

"It's Kitty!" she blurted out.

"What about Kitty?" he asked lazily, as if his mind were on other things.

"She's in love with you."

"Nonsense."

"It's true! How could she not be—I mean, I'm certain of it. I saw"—ashamed to admit to spying on Kitty, however inadvertently, Celia lowered her head. "She told me so."

He smiled again, apparently unable to take the notion seriously. "What she probably said was that she adores me. Kitty adores kittens and the gardener's old setter bitch and the youngest kitchen maid—and me. Any creature that will curl up in her lap and hang on her every word. Surely you know that by now?"

Celia could see that he would not believe her if she went on in this muddled way, neither explaining herself nor able to ask him directly what his feelings were. Her confusion made her angry at herself. Almost unaware that she was doing it, she transferred that anger to him.

"Surely you must know by now that there is more to it than that?" she countered. "Kitty loves you, I know, but she does not wish to reveal her true feelings for fear of your laughing at them in just that way."

"How do you know this?"

Celia hesitated. "I saw—a letter. Kitty had dropped it on the floor of her room. It spoke of *a castle by the sea*."

"And you thought it was meant for me?"

"I'm certain of it. Kitty is so—well, romantically minded that you must seem to her the embodiment of the heroes from those novels she reads so much. I thought you were going to elope with her—to run away from a betrothal she cannot bring herself to break, just as the Proctors ran away from Lavinia's unhappy marriage."

"Oh, good God." He sounded as if he had just tasted something unpleasant. "How can such an intelligent woman be so blind? I had no notion you had such a fertile imagination, or I would have tried much harder to channel it in another direction."

"What—what do you mean?"

"I mean that I am not in love with Kitty. I never was, and she knows it. That's why she felt able to confide in me."

Celia remembered then those little tête-à-têtes she had caught them in—or imagined she had. "But . . . what were you talking about so earnestly that morning in the garden? And at supper just the other night, and—and what was Kitty doing in the library last night?"

He raised his brows. "Well, it seems you aren't precisely blind—just blinkered. I don't remember what specifically we talked about on those occasions, and I'm damned if I'd explain it if I could. Kitty asked my help with something, and I tried to give it. That's all."

"Was it something to do with Julian, then?"

"Celia—no, damn it, I won't explain myself here in a stable, where someone may interrupt us at any moment! Besides, you deserve to remain in ignorance a little longer to reflect on your folly."

She could not tell if he were joking now, for his tone was light, but the look in his eyes was stormy. She gazed up at him to try to understand what he was saying, but his face had moved suddenly out of her vision. It was an instant before she realised the reason for this, because he had lowered his head towards hers and was touching her lips with his.

She made a move away from him, but he caught her waist and held her close to him while he kissed her neck, murmuring *"and Celia has undone me"* before he found her lips again. He tasted slightly of salt, she thought irrelevantly. Then the taste on her lips sweetened and she could not resist parting them a little to savour more. She was being selfish, she knew, but his mouth did feel delicious on hers.

Perhaps just this once, she thought, giving in and moving her head to let him kiss her again. It would be nice to be the princess herself for a little while, to imagine that she was the kind of woman men like Nicky Lambert really wanted to make love to. *Tomorrow* she thought, *tomorrow I'll be sensible.*

A noise behind them suddenly recalled the groom's presence, and he let her go. He was breathing hard, and he looked at her in a way that made her blush and turn away. She caught Julian's eye over Nicky's shoulder and for an instant thought she saw him smile. Then she pushed Nicky from her and ran past Julian out of the stable.

The sunshine in the stable yard hit her almost like a blow, and she halted abruptly. She could hear nothing from inside for a moment. Then there was a horse's neighing, the jingle of harness, and the gentlemen came around the side of the building already mounted. Julian, in the lead, raised his riding crop to his hat and smiled, but Nicky did not look at her. His expression was grim, as if he did not trust her to wait for him, but had no choice other than to go with Julian . . .

Only then did Celia remember she had not asked him what he was doing in the stable.

"Where are you going?" she called out.

But they were already out of earshot.

=14=

CELIA WATCHED NICKY and Julian until they were out of sight down the lane, unaware until she began to breathe again and relaxed her posture that she had been standing there in the yard for several moments with her hands crossed over her heart.

Was he angry with her? A new fear assailed her as the memory of Harry's impatience on the day he died came back to her. Was Nicky going to go off and do something foolish as well, only because she had been foolish enough to be provoking?

But no—Nicky's kiss when he left her had not held that kind of anger. It was impatience he felt, nothing more. *You deserve to remain in ignorance a little longer to reflect on your folly*, he had said. And he was right.

It was several moments nonetheless before she became composed enough again to move without stumbling, and she was several steps closer to the house before her thoughts stopped tripping over one another. She had been so sure that the evidence she had so painstakingly gathered pointed to only one conclusion. Yet, in a matter of minutes Nicky had destroyed all of her certainties. Could she have simply mistaken the first clue—his flirting with Kitty—and then built her whole flimsy case on top of it?

And what were Nicky's feelings towards her? She must have mistaken those, too, from the start. No wonder he was angry at her! If he had been the one to believe that—well, that she was secretly in love with Julian, for example, would she not have been angry at his blindness?

She had to smile at that. She and Julian were simply too much alike to treat each other any other way than warily. Nicky, on the other hand, was so unlike either of them that the notion of his being in love with her had never crossed her mind, despite the things he had said to her—things that made her blush even more now that she realised what they really meant. She allowed herself to dwell on them anew, and the implications pleased her very much indeed in a way that thinking about Harry had never done. She had loved Harry, certainly, but she had always been a little on edge with him, waiting for something to go wrong. Somehow she knew instinctively that life with Nicky Lambert would run very smoothly, very comfortably—for a very long time.

And yet her thoughts would not let her dwell on that rosy picture for long. Marrying Nicky would mean uprooting the life she had here and had come to love. Would she be able to do that, to give up her comforts, her freedom? One did not lightly foresake such things, even for a castle by the sea—at least, not until one was ready to put away the treasures of the past and begin collecting new memories. Somehow that idea seemed comforting—a way to have, or to hold, the best of both her worlds.

Celia smiled to herself as she crossed the lawn to go into the house again by the sun-parlour door. Then she suddenly saw Kitty come running out of the garden, where she had apparently abandoned Sir Phineas. She hesitated and glanced around her as if she did not know why she was there.

"Where have they gone?" she asked Celia.

"I don't know," Celia said, taking Kitty's arm. The fine muscles beneath the soft skin were unusually tense. Celia knew that she would have to confess the error of her ways to Kitty now, but she did not know how to begin. "Was there something you wanted to say to Nicky?"

"To Nicky? No. No, it's Julian. Did he say anything to you, Celia?"

Celia frowned. "Julian? Oh, dear, I'm afraid we are talking at cross-purposes. Let's go inside and try to explain ourselves, shall we?"

Kitty stamped her foot and, seeming not to hear her, said, "Why doesn't he tell me what's wrong? He has always confided in me before. Now, just when something is really troubling him—"

Much to Celia's astonishment, Kitty burst into tears and threw her arms around her friend. "Oh, Celia, why does he not trust me, when I love him so much!"

Celia's heart stopped for a moment, unable to stand the suspense. For an instant, she thought she had heard all her own fears dashed to nothing, but she must be certain.

"Who, darling?"

Sniffling, Kitty pushed herself away to look at Celia. "Why—Julian, of course. Who else is there?"

Celia almost laughed with relief, but Kitty would not have understood. Indeed, she herself did not now understand her own folly. Nicky was perfectly right. How could she have been so blind?

Kitty reached into her pocket for a handkerchief and blew her nose. Meanwhile, Celia attempted to marshall her thoughts and to consider Kitty's feelings as well. Celia suggested that they go into the sun parlour, where they would be private. Once installed there, however, she found herself no more articulate than before. Fortunately, Kitty had no such difficulty.

"I suppose it should not matter," she said, as if she had been speaking for some time. Celia supposed that she had been mulling all this over in her mind for days now, and it all came out in a rush. "I know that Julian loves me, even if he rarely shows it or says so, but I cannot blame Lavinia for running away from her husband all those years ago because he would not show her any affection. Of course, the cases are not precisely the same because she did not really love James . . ."

"Is that why you invited the Proctors here?" Celia had to ask.

"Not precisely," Kitty said. "I had hoped they would prove

to be as much in love with each other now as then, and although it did not at first seem possible, they have proved indeed to be even a better example to put before Julian than I could have dreamed. Only he does not see it. He is so—so stubborn!"

Light dawned on Celia. "Is that what you meant, on the steamboat that day, about the Proctors proving inspiring? You were talking about Julian, not Nicky."

Kitty sniffed one last time into her handkerchief, then folded it neatly and put it in her pocket. "Yes, of course. Sometimes it seemed to me that Julian would never really marry me, although I tried so hard to be patient," she said, revealing her true impatience by getting up and beginning to pace the floor.

Celia smiled. "Perhaps you were right when you said he may simply be reluctant to accept his good fortune. He does not believe he deserves it. I know I often felt that way about Harry, and now . . ."

She broke off, reluctant yet to think of Nicky in those terms.

"But why not?" Kitty demanded, her mind still on her own stubborn love. "What has he done *not* to deserve to be happy? It is not as if I haven't made my own feelings clear. I even had to ask *him* to marry me!"

Kitty left off pacing the room and with a sigh, sat down again on the chair next to Celia. "I used to write him love letters," she said, "to remind him of it, but he never answered them. I think they embarrassed him so I don't send them anymore."

"You don't *send* them?" Celia asked, as a revealing thought struck her. "Do you still write them then?"

"Oh, yes, all the time. It makes me feel better to write them, but I throw them in the fireplace."

"Did one of them—forgive me, darling, but I found it on the floor and could not help glancing at it—did one of them speak of a castle by the sea?"

"Most of them did. When I was small, you see, I imagined myself a princess in a castle by the sea. That was Hardwicke

Manor, of course—and Julian was the prince." Kitty looked down at her hands and said, in the most grown-up way Celia had ever heard from her, "He still is."

It occurred to Celia that the picturesque poses and deliberately fairy-story mannerisms that Kitty adopted and she and Nicky had laughed at—even including her reluctance to be seen doing anything so unprincesslike as household chores—must have been part of Kitty's attempt to convince Julian that she really was his dream princess come true. Celia rose to kiss Kitty's cheek and give her a light hug.

"And you have never loved—anyone else?" she asked gently.

"There was never anyone else."

"Not even Nicky Lambert?"

Kitty smiled. "Nicky's in love with you, goose. I knew it, and he knew I knew. That is why it was safe to flirt with him, you see. Only you did not know."

"Perhaps it was jealousy on my part, but I was always seeing you and Nicky together, flirting and sharing little secrets and—well, I don't know what else. What were you talking about?"

Having unburdened her own heart, Kitty showed renewed sympathy now for her sister-in-law. "I'm sorry, dearest, if it worried you. I confess I hadn't considered that. At first, it's true, I thought that flirting with Nicky might make Julian jealous so that he would—well, I don't know what precisely. Insist on our being married at once, perhaps, or even call Nicky out." She smiled. "Once I thought that would be the height of romance. But Julian only thought that it was a good thing for me to have a friend like Nicky who would give me the little compliments Julian could not, which was not at all what I intended of course. So then I confided in Nicky and asked him to help me make Julian understand that I truly love him."

"Did he?"

"Well, he spoke to Julian as best he could about it. I don't know if it helped. Then Nicky told me that Julian had something else on his mind and that when that had been settled perhaps he would be less preoccupied and would listen to me. Then Nicky could get on with winning you." Kitty gave Celia a sly glance. "Most recently, you know, darling, Nicky has thought of nothing but you and he has been absolutely no use to me. I ought to be very much annoyed with you."

Celia flushed and managed to joke feebly that as it had been Kitty's professed plan to make a match between her sister-in-law and Nicky Lambert from the start, she ought to be glad it had happened with no effort on her part. Kitty, who seemed to have recovered her good sense more quickly, only laughed and said, "Well! When the gentlemen return from wherever they have dared to go without us, we will have to undo all this confusion, won't we?"

The gentlemen, meanwhile, were riding over the downs, approaching the Tyler Farm. Like the weather, which had turned unexpectedly from warm and sunny to cloudy and threatening, Julian grew increasingly abstracted as they drew nearer their destination. Nicky finally gave up trying to make polite conversation, which met with only monosyllabic responses.

"We don't know the man is even alive," Nicky had said as they set off from the manor.

"I must be certain of that," Julian replied. "I don't mean to imply that I wish the man dead, but I cannot rest easily again until I am certain of my own position. I had not realised I had taken it so much for granted."

"Understandable, I'm sure," Nicky remarked dryly, "when everything was left to you unconditionally by your father's will."

"I do not refer only to the manor, you know."

"I collect you are speaking of Kitty then. But your hold on her heart is, if anything, more secure than on your home. Surely you know that."

"If it were only for your telling me so I must surely know it by now. But Hardwicke Manor has always meant a great deal to Kitty."

"Naturally enough. It is like a second home to her—her first, even now, if truth be told."

"But it is not just the house. The manor represents something more to Kitty. It is her girlhood dream come true. She sees me as a prince in a castle, you see, and I am not at all certain that I would look so princely in her eyes without the castle."

"Then you do not know Kitty nearly so well as you think."

Glancing at his friend, Julian smiled and asked, "Not so well as you, I suppose?"

"Very likely not," Nicky said, unperturbed by any possible misinterpretation of his words. "My vision of her is not clouded by self-doubt and imaginary obstacles to what will be a very happy marriage when you finally do marry her. I trust, by the way, that you will not postpone the wedding yet again? Indeed, I strongly suggest you move the date forward instead. Otherwise I may very well have to elope with Kitty to make you chase after us, and you would not at all care to be married over the anvil at Gretna Green, I assure you. Very undignified it would be."

Julian had to laugh. "I do not dare ask how you know so much about runaway marriages. But very well, if what we learn today does not turn everything upside down, I promise I will marry Kitty as soon as it is possible to do so with a modicum of dignity."

"And if bad news awaits us?"

Julian sobered quickly and drew his horse briefly to a halt to look out over the countryside. They had reached the top of the long rise from the sea and now had only rolling green farmland ahead of them. A slight break in the clouds allowed a shaft of sunlight through, but there was no telling if the break would widen or close again.

"I hope I can meet such a possibility with dignity as well," Julian said. "But I am not at all certain of that."

15

BEFORE JULIAN RETURNED, the afternoon had cast long shadows in the library, where Kitty and Celia had taken up their vigil when the sun parlour became too cool for comfort. Kitty heard his footsteps first and looked up quickly from the book she had not been reading to stare hopefully at the door.

Julian came through it, alone and looking tired, but at the same time somehow refreshed. Celia realised only then that she had not seen him without a crease of concern in his forehead for some days. He stopped, surprised to find them there, but after a moment he smiled at Kitty. As if this were some sort of signal, Kitty jumped up and flung herself into his arms.

Celia waited as patiently as she could, fighting back her rising concern that Nicky had not returned also—perhaps he was detained in the stables?—until Kitty loosened her hold on Julian sufficiently to allow him to speak. He had anticipated Celia's question.

"Nicky sends his regrets, Celia, and begs you to forgive him, but the instant we reached the stables here he received a message from Woodbridge and was obliged to set out again with only a change of horse. He gave me a note for you."

Julian handed her the paper—the same note had been sent to Nicky, for on one side it read, "Come home at once. Father not expected to last the night. Mary."

On the other side, folded inwards, Nicky had scrawled:

"As you see, my dear, I must go at once. Forgive me and please wait for me. I must speak to you when I return. God knows when that will be. N."

It was several minutes before Celia was able to tear her mind away from this missive to find Julian's eyes on her.

"Did you know his father was ill?" Julian asked, unaffected sympathy in his voice. Celia nodded.

"Then you understand it will be best if it ends quickly. We must all pray for that."

"But where were you both *before* that, Julian?" Kitty asked, pulling impatiently on his sleeve. He put his arm around her shoulder and smiled down at her.

"Patience, Kitten. We are only waiting for the Proctors, who will wish to hear the story with you."

"Why are you being so mysterious? What have the Proctors to do with anything?"

Julian laughed, surprising Celia again. Apparently, whatever mysterious mission had taken him and Nicky Lambert away so abruptly had led to a happy outcome, but she could not imagine what it might have been.

"I think perhaps I should leave you to fret in the dark, Kitty, for bringing all this worry on me by inviting the Proctors here in the first place. However, since they have also provided the key to the puzzle, I must forgive you—this time."

"What puzzle?" Kitty demanded, stamping her slippered foot on the thick carpet.

Fortunately, there was a knock on the door just then, which served to relieve Kitty's frustration for a few minutes, and Jeffreys admitted Sir Phineas and Lady Proctor. Sir Phineas held his wife's hand firmly on his arm, as if to support her should she suddenly fall away in a dead faint. Lavinia, although she looked pale enough to do just that, nevertheless stood straight and looked directly at Julian, her eyes questioning but not fearful.

Julian went to her immediately and took her hands in his. She looked up at him and seemed to understand something that was as yet a mystery to Celia. Then Sir Phineas, still treating Lavinia as if she were made of porcelain, guided her to a chair and pulled out his handkerchief to dab her eyes gently. Celia and Kitty sat down together on the sofa. Julian took up a position in front of the fireplace and addressed them all in a voice so soothing that at first Celia's attention wandered, as her mind tried to picture where Nicky might be now and what he might be feeling. *Was he unhappy—or relieved? Was he thinking of her? If only she could be with him.*

So caught up was she in her imaginings that she scarcely heard Julian say, a moment later, "This in a small way also concerns you, Celia, so please hear me out."

She looked at him, startled, trying to clear her mind and concentrate on what he was saying, but he had already turned his gaze to Kitty.

"First I must apologise to you, Kitty, and Celia, too, for going away so mysteriously this morning, but the fact is that I had no idea what I would find or even what I was looking for. In the end what I found was indeed not what I was looking for."

He paused, then took a small parcel from his pocket. Handing it to Kitty to open, he went on, "We did not find the man we were looking for—Lucas Tyler."

He glanced at Celia. "Does that name mean anything to you, Mrs. Morland?"

Celia frowned. It did have a familiar sound, but she could not place it and said so.

"No one could expect you to remember it, but Lucas Tyler is the name of the man who was drowned when the search party was sent out to look for Harry Morland. Harry's body was found soon after, so very likely, if you heard the name, Celia, you would have forgotten it again in your grief."

She felt Kitty's hand rest comfortingly on her own, and that did indeed banish the quick stab of memory that had pained her for an instant. She smiled gratefully at Kitty.

"Lucas Tyler was your son, Lavinia," Julian went on, looking at Lady Proctor. "The family confirmed that. What you said the other day was true. Lucas had a good life with the

Tylers and could not have been a better man in any other circumstances, however luxurious. He had not only a loving father and mother, but a wife. She, too, died young, but not before giving Lucas a daughter."

"A daughter!" Lavinia looked up eagerly. "Then she would be—my granddaughter?"

Celia thought it odd that at the idea of being a grandmother Lavinia actually looked younger, but so she did. Kitty, who had unwrapped the parcel Julian gave her, rose to hand Lavinia the miniature inside. Everyone but Julian crowded around to have a look.

"She's very pretty," Kitty said.

"She looks like Lavinia," said Sir Phineas, with some truth, Celia agreed. The miniature looked like the old portrait of Lavinia as a bride, which still hung in that corner of the picture gallery where Celia had first seen it.

"What is her name?" Lavinia asked.

"Barbara. She is just turned fourteen."

Lavinia gazed at the miniature and dabbed her eyes again before glancing questioningly up at Phineas.

"Does she know—did you tell the Tylers everything?" Phineas asked.

"I brought them up to date, yes. I did not think it my place to make promises on your behalf, but I am certain that if you wished to offer to help the girl in some way, they would not object. Their means are modest, despite James's provision and Lucas's hard work. I suspect that they view the girl rather as an exotic butterfly that has somehow flown in their window by mistake. I daresay they would be grateful to give her a better life—even to let you adopt her, if you and Lavinia would like that."

Sir Phineas nodded. "We will provide for her."

"Very well." Julian smiled then and looked around at the expectant faces. "That is all I have to say."

"No, it isn't," Kitty said, coming to Julian's side. "Now that I have all these witnesses conveniently by, Julian, I insist that you set our wedding date once and for all!"

Julian laughed, for once unembarrassed by her public

demonstrativeness. "I thought we did have one set."

"Not *that* one. It is so far in the future that I shall very likely go into a decline before it ever arrives. Set another."

Julian gazed down at her fondly. "Would next week be too far away?"

"Well, it isn't tomorrow, but I suppose it is a vast improvement."

With that Kitty put her arms around him, and Julian submitted once again to being kissed while Lavinia dabbed her eyes and Phineas silently applauded. Then, since they would obviously not be missed, Celia and the Proctors slipped quietly out of the room.

When Sir Phineas had closed the door behind himself, Julian pulled Kitty closer and kissed her properly.

"That was very—definite—of you," Kitty said when she had got her breath back.

"Now that I find myself in full possession not only of my wits, but of my house and everything else I ever promised you, I think I have a right to be confident at last," he said, smiling.

Kitty stepped out of his embrace long enough to look up at him with a thoroughly exasperated expression.

"Julian, why could you never understand that I would love you in whatever hovel we had to call our castle? That is the one thing you have always been justified in feeling confident of, yet you never would."

"I'm sorry, my love. I will try to do better—if you will make do without the hovel."

Kitty laughed. "Well, I do admit to just the smallest partiality for luxuries if there are any to be had."

"I shall shower you with them."

"And you will put up with my little fancies about castles and such?"

"I will do my best to join in."

"Good. Then we can be married with every expectation of living happily ever after!"

The moon had taken possession of the sun parlour. Celia

sat in the wicker chair facing the door and gazed out over the lawn. She should not expect him back tonight. It was too soon. Yet she could not bring herself to go to bed.

She wished she could be with him, to comfort him. He had said, or at least indicated, that there was no feeling left between him and his father. Still—it *was* his father. Very likely in the end the feeling would return, and Nicky would be sorry to say good-bye.

She wondered again at her own foolishness. She had to believe that Kitty meant it when she said there had never been anyone for her but Julian. Their plans, confirmed over dinner, to be married at once had proved that. The only reason Celia ever had to suppose Kitty in love with Nicky was that she was so in love with him herself that she could not imagine indifference to him on any woman's part. Now, of course, she had the dreadful suspicion that she would never again countenance any woman looking at him admiringly. She wondered idly if she would be capable of enough sheer feminine possessiveness to despatch a rival with either skill or wit. Certainly she had never been put to the test with Harry—not because no other woman ever looked at him, but because Celia had been amused rather than incensed by these encounters. Somehow she knew it would not be the same with Nicky.

Nothing was the same with Nicky. She had been in love with Harry, it was true, but there had been little substance behind it. She had not loved him as well. She knew instinctively that Nicky Lambert would be all things to her, and she would be as much to him, even if they had only just begun to explore all the delightful ways they might come to know each other.

The large fern by the door rustled gently in the breeze, and Celia looked up to see a shadow fall across the doorway and to hear a familiar, welcome voice say, "I thought I might find you here."

She said nothing, but rose to walk across the room into his embrace. He hesitated for a moment, then gathered her close.

"I've just got back," he murmured, "I must be filthy."

"It doesn't matter."

But she knew from the change in his voice that it did. This was a much subdued Nicky, his voice lower, his manner as sober as she had ever known it. She stepped back to gaze at him. The hazel eyes were clouded.

"Is he—?"

"He's dead, yes. He died just before I got there. I didn't even have a chance to . . . not that it matters, I suppose. There wouldn't have been any more to say than there has ever been between us. It's just that . . . I wish . . ."

He took a deep breath then, and she could feel a shudder pass through him. She put her arms around him again, and he clung to her fiercely. She could feel his sobs but did not attempt to comfort him. She was simply happy that he had come to her to release his feelings.

After a while, he loosened his grip and said calmly, "I'm sorry. You didn't know him. It is nothing to do with you."

"But it is," she said, looking up at him. "It must be. If you cannot come to me—bring me your sorrows as well as your smiles—what hope have we?"

He frowned, but his hazel eyes had cleared, she thought, as if he were coming back to life. "I did feel—when I got to Woodbridge, I wished I had brought you with me. It was impossible, of course, but I had the idea that you would have come, even have risked being thought an intruder, if I had asked you."

"I would."

"Mary—my sister—wants to meet you. I told her about you the last time I was there. So you would not have been an intruder, in any case."

"Unless she did not care for me."

"Impossible!" he said, and now the laughter began to creep back into his eyes, too.

"Not at all. I am not like you and Kitty. Not everyone instantly adores me. Julian barely tolerates me."

"Oh—Julian!" Nicky dismissed his best friend as beside the point. "You and Julian are too much alike. That's your trouble. You're both too honest. Neither of you can flatter enough to inspire any softness in the other."

"Then I wonder you put up with me. If I am so honest, I must have insulted you any number of times."

"Oh, you have. But I can be stubborn, too—and persistent."

"I was so foolish, about you and Kitty—"

"Yes, why did you persist in thinking we were going to elope, by the way?"

"I thought that was the reason she invited the Proctors here—because they had run away to be married and Kitty wanted to do the same."

"I haven't a notion why she invited the Proctors, but I'm certain it had nothing to do with me. Unless, of course, it had to do with you and me. I must confess, I never thought of that. I've been very slow to take the hint, I see."

"You and me?"

"My love, have you been drinking Henrietta's tea again? I am convinced it slows the mental processes to a crawl and that even the quickest-witted of persons is not immune to its effect." He laughed but left off teasing her to say, "What about Kitty, incidentally? Was she able to persuade Julian to elope with her?"

Celia laughed. "Not precisely. They have compromised by moving the wedding up to next week."

"Good. We will still be here for it."

"*We?*"

"Before we leave for Jamaica, that is. It will take at least that long to pack, I should imagine."

"But what shall I do in Jamaica?" Celia persisted, finding a certain delight in being a tease, after all.

"Walk barefoot on the beach, and fill the house with flowers, and look at the sea all day long. And be my wife—all day and all night long." He looked down at her questioningly as she seemed to consider this idea. Then, as if to be sure she had understood quite clearly, he said again, "Will you marry me, Celia?"

"Yes," she said, sighing. "I suppose I must."

He laughed and asked sternly, "Must, madam? Why *must*, pray?"

"Because I love you, of course."

His eyes darkened at that. She could hear the intake of his breath before he pulled her close again and kissed her at last, lingeringly, on the mouth and the back of her neck and below her ear and again on the mouth. A delicious warmth spread through her that she would have liked to bask in forever—if only the moonlight were not fading and if only she did not feel herself becoming too weak to hold onto him any longer.

"Oh . . . do stop."

With some effort he loosened his hold on her—not quite enough to let her fall, for she would not let him move that far away.

"By all means, let us be sensible."

She smiled. "Oh, well—not all that sensible. I am beginning to see that sense has been very little use to me in the past. Although, of course, if you wish a sensible wife, I will do my best to be accommodating."

"I doubt that your sensible English habits will be of much use in Jamaica, so you had best jettison them here."

"Oh, yes—you did say you lived in Jamaica, didn't you?"

Sober again, he looked closely at her. "Shall you dislike it very much to leave your home?"

"I don't know. Do you have a castle there? Kitty says I must insist on a castle."

He laughed, relieved. "Well, it is certainly a large building, and it is near the sea. I fear any other resemblance to Hardwicke Manor is of the slightest. On the other hand, all the rooms are sun parlours, and there is a wide veranda around the entire house. You may lie in a hammock to drink your tea."

"That certainly doesn't sound very sensible."

"Not in the least. Shall we be married here or there?"

"Perhaps we should elope, since no one else seems to

want to. I could leave a note on the mantel, as Lavinia did."

"A very fine, unsensible idea. I shall consult Sir Phineas on how to go about it. Afterwards."

"After what?"

"After I have kissed you again. Once or twice."

"Or even," said Celia, sensibly, "three or four times."